I0520131

Horrid

Honeymoon

Cyberworld Publishing

Cyberworld Publishing

www.CyberworldPublishing.com

Cyberworld Publishing
Jindalee St
Toronto, Australia

Horrid

Honeymoon

Charlotte Diamond Mysteries Eight

Olivia Stowe

Table of Contents

Chapter One: Right off the Bat.................................... 7

Chapter Two: Day One; The Baltimore Cruise Line Pier . 25

Chapter Three: Even Before the Ship Sails........................ 35

Chapter Four: Steaming Down the Chesapeake Bay 47

Chapter Five: Exposure at the Pool 61

Chapter Six: The Murder Cabin 73

Chapter Seven: Fire on the Water! 77

Chapter Eight: Up the Creek Without a Paddle................. 85

Chapter Nine: Dark Sanctuary.. 91

Chapter Ten: Putting the Last Mystery to Bed................. 105

About the Author 115

Chapter One: Right off the Bat

"March is the cruelest month."

"You keep saying that, Charlotte love. It's just a snow flurry. It's not like we've had blizzards this month or anything."

"It's six days into spring. You've spent most of the last few decades in Southern California. You don't know what a snow cloud looks like. Look up there. We're in for a foot or more of the stuff."

"Don't be so pessimistic, Charlotte," Brenda said. "We're into spring. How bad could it get? And stop pulling at your suit top. You look fine."

"I look like an upholstered couch, and you know it," Charlotte answered.

Brenda put her arm around Charlotte and kissed her on the cheek. "Well, you're my upholstered couch."

"Ouch," Charlotte said.

"Just trying to loosen you up. I told you. You look great. Jitters? Second thoughts?"

"Jitters? Of course, and don't tell me you aren't having them too, under that oh so cool Grace Kelly exterior," Charlotte answered. "Second thoughts?" she continued. "Absolutely not. I just can't get it done fast enough. And I'm worried about this snow. We have a cruise ship to catch in Baltimore tomorrow."

"The ship isn't the important part. Neither is the snow," Brenda said in a soft voice. "All that matters is the ceremony. And even that it mostly icing on the cake on what we already have together. We're here and everyone who really matters for that is here too. It will all work out beautifully. But if it doesn't, it doesn't, and it doesn't matter. All that will matter is that we're married. And stop pulling at your suit top. You look terrific."

"Not compared with you. Why did I go with the green brocade? Your white silk looks elegant. I don't think you could look anything but elegant. I look like an elephant that fell in through a window and got tangled in the drapes."

Brenda didn't say anything. She just kept hugging her spouse to be and patting her on the arm. She understood how nervous Charlotte was. Charlotte had been married before, conventionally, and it had been a disaster. Brenda hadn't been married before; instead she'd been in a previous same-sex relationship. She'd already faced all of the problems that went with it, so she had fewer reasons to be nervous about this than Charlotte had.

The two were standing at a window of the parlor of the Episcopal church rectory just a couple of blocks from their Hopewell-on-the-Choptank federal mansion, the former main house of the riverside plantation that had covered this region of Maryland from the seventeenth century and that Brenda Boynton's family had lived in from its construction. Brenda herself, though, had spent more than the previous three decades in Hollywood, where, as Brenda Brandon, she had risen to be one of the world's most beloved leading movie actresses. She had returned to Hopewell under a cloud, suspected of having murdered her significant other, the Hollywood costume designer, Helga Lund. And back home on the banks of the Choptank River, emptying into the Chesapeake Bay, was where she had met Charlotte Diamond.

Charlotte had recently moved here after both a divorce and having retired from the Annapolis office of the FBI as a senior investigator. The two had clicked and Charlotte subsequently had been instrumental in clearing Brenda of being a murder suspect. More than two years of living through diversity and shared mystery and danger had only deepened the affection the two had for each other. The State of Maryland having recently

8

passed same-sex marriage legislation had led to today. In the wake of the law change, Brenda proposed and Charlotte answered, "Why the hell not?" Initially Charlotte thought Brenda was joking, but Brenda made quite clear that she wasn't—that she really was proposing a legal marriage between the two.

So, they were getting married in the small Episcopal church in the village of Hopewell—evidently during a spring snowfall.

Candles were in the sconces lining the stone walls of the small church as the only illumination, in addition to cascading candelabras on the altar, as Brenda and Charlotte walked down the center aisle, hand in hand. Floodlights on the exterior of the church lit up the most charming aspect of the chapel, its colorful stained-glass windows. The near emptiness of the church belied the prominence the two held in the village, where Brenda's family had held the most prominent position for centuries over and above her reputation as a major movie star and being the beneficiary of the village's principal business, the recently opened Curtain Call retirement community for movie industry employees. Charlotte was not much less a significant part of Hopewell, even though she was a recent resident. She not only was the town's mayor but she also held a reputation of her own as a premier sleuth. Thus it could be seen as unusual—and perhaps a bit disturbing—that the whole town hadn't turned out for the wedding. Other than the odd collection of folks and beasts standing at the altar before the church's minister, Don Dunkel, two lone women sitting in the last pew, and a photographer, a role taken by the village barber, Walt Miller, standing at the back, waiting to take the post-ceremony photos, the church was empty.

This was not a commentary of disapproval of the two women marrying, though. It was the result of an agreement between the two women being married. Both of them wanted a small, private ceremony—the point of this to both was not to make the splash of a public statement—and neither one of them wanted to hurt or insult the many friends and townspeople who wanted to celebrate their nuptials. Thus, although the ceremony itself was to be very private, a lavish wedding reception was already under way some distance away at the Tidewater Inn in

Easton, Maryland. The wedding party was to be driven there by limousine at the conclusion of this elegant, yet simple ceremony. Brenda and Charlotte were to spend the night at the Tidewater Inn following the reception and then be driven to the Baltimore cruise line pier the next morning, along with their wedding party, for a seven-day honeymoon cruise to the Bahamas. Neither woman had wanted more of a trip than that, but both wanted to celebrate in some way. They couldn't think of any better way than taking the human members of their wedding party on the cruise with them. Strangely enough, the major problem with that plan was the need to leave their nonhuman family home.

Standing at the altar rail, and beaming at Charlotte and Brenda as, eschewing tradition, the two walked down the aisle arm in arm, was, on Brenda's side, her son, Tony Trice. Tony was a "dreamboat-role" movie star and had been in several movies with Brenda as part of an ensemble with more than a dozen popular movies to its credit. It had been not much more than a year since Tony had been revealed to be the son Brenda had in secret out of wedlock before she had come to Hollywood to make her mark on the silver screen. Although she had left Tony behind, she hadn't abandoned him. She had followed and enhanced his life and, when he had shown acting talent, she had made sure that he was offered parts in Hollywood that would highlight his natural abilities.

Tony was there as part of the wedding party not to give Brenda away—everyone had recognized that in her late fifties and as successful as she'd been in life through her own efforts, she needed no one to give her away—but to be by her side at this happy occasion.

On Charlotte's side were her brother, Chance Diamond, a Williamsburg, Virginia, doctor and Charlotte's only living relative, and his wife, Marilyn Diamond, who was a United Methodist minister. The two were as much Brenda's close friends as Charlotte's relatives, as three years previously the four of them had shared a memorable Christmas-season trip down the Rhine River that had been fraught with intrigue and mystery and Brenda had found the senior Diamonds to be delightful travel companions.

The added touch of "strange" to the ceremony was the presence at the rail of two dogs, who both Charlotte and Brenda considered to be their "kids." On Charlotte's side sat Sam, a Siberian husky Charlotte had inherited from her first Hopewell neighbors. On Brenda's side was their other dog, Rocket, a boxer, which the two had acquired by default when another neighbor, a supposedly retired CIA official, Winston Engleton, had feigned his own death and disappeared to the West Coast. Engleton had left his dog behind in Charlotte's care as evidence of his death, but he had known full well that she would willingly add the boxer to her family.

The two dogs were the reason one of the women sitting at the back of the church was there. Brenda and Charlotte's housekeeper, Bea Helgerson, would be staying in Hopewell with Sam and Rocket. Bea was as devoted to the dogs as Brenda and Charlotte were, and the women couldn't take the dogs on the cruise with them.

The other woman sitting at the back was Tony's current girlfriend—and the woman both Brenda and Charlotte hoped Tony would settle down with—the popular professional tennis star, Michelle Minor. Michelle had demurred from the offer to stand at the altar rail beside Tony, since she was not family, but she would be cruising with the wedding party.

The women reached the altar and without further ado, Father Don Dunkel began the simple, short ceremony: "Friends we are gathered together to join . . ."

Both women began to tear up at that point—not because of the emotion of joining in matrimony with each other. Brenda and Charlotte had considered themselves married for some time before the State of Maryland had passed a law permitting them to do so legally. Their emotional response to voicing the simple words of the wedding vows they had agreed to with Don Dunkel were more in recognition of the priest's willingness to sacrifice his own traditional views on marriage to perform a ceremony joining two women in marriage. Both women recognized how deeply this willingness to suspend his own beliefs reflected his respect and affection for them. And, in turn, they had insisted that he be the one to conduct the ceremony—and that the ceremony be conducted in his church—even though Marilyn Diamond could have just as effectively done the deed for them in the parlor of their home.

Sam and Rocket were being as good as gold. Both dogs were sitting quietly and following their mistresses with their eyes all the way down the aisle. They neither barked nor disrupted the ceremony in any way but looked on with solemn expressions as if they fully understood how significant this occasion was—and that Brenda and Charlotte and not they were the center of attention for these brief moments.

The vows over, Brenda and Charlotte simply turned and, with the wedding party following them, walked back down the aisle. At this point, the dogs, in consort, broke discipline and followed along at the sides of their mistresses, waging their tails in satisfaction and joy.

There had been no music. Although Don Dunkel had performed the ceremony, he had requested that he be excused from the reception, and, understanding how difficult it had been for him to perform a same-sex marriage ceremony, the two women had diplomatically not pressed him to attend. He would have been the one to drive the organist, Mary Sparks, who was also his housekeeper, to the reception, though. So, Brenda and Charlotte suggested that she go ahead with other residents of the village and they would just forgo music. The ceremony would only last for a few minutes anyway.

Tony, somewhat tongue in cheek, had suggested that Brenda, an accomplished singer, sing something a cappella, but Brenda had just swatted him and said she'd be too choked up to manage it. Until then, she had been acting like there was nothing tear-worthy in such an occasion, but she blushed at this acknowledgment that the ceremony would deeply affect her.

The photo session lasted longer than the ceremony did, as Hopewell resident Walt Miller, the village's barber shop owner, was both a fussy and not a particularly adept photographer.

The surprise was how much it could snow in the period of time the ceremony and photo session took during a March snowstorm in the Mid Atlantic region. When the wedding party reached the church doors, it was only with difficulty that they managed to get them open, such was the power of the wind lashing at the front of the building. Brenda and Charlotte were nearly blown back into the arms of Chance and Tony, and the dogs let out their first yelps of the afternoon.

"Flurries, you said," Charlotte muttered as she supported the lighter-weight movie star, who had been blown into Charlotte's arms—not that Charlotte objected to that.

"Well, maybe a bit more than that," Brenda answered with a game smile and her patented tinkling laugh. She obviously was determined not to let anything ruin this occasion.

There must have been six inches of snow that had dropped since Charlotte spied the flurries beginning from the rectory window. It was sticking to the street in front of the church and was already drifting.

"We'll have to make a dash for the limousine," Brenda called out over the howl of the wind.

"What limousine?" Charlotte called back.

There was supposed to be a stretch limousine, driven by Billy Zirkel, the young man who now owned, in partnership with Brenda and Charlotte, and operated the village gas station farther up the street the church was on. But there was no limousine waiting outside the church entrance. And there was no Billy Zirkel either. Or so it seemed at first.

But then, as Chance Diamond and Tony Trice moved out in front of Brenda and Charlotte to give them some protection from the swirling snow and biting wind, they heard moaning from the bushes to the right of the church doors.

Tony moved to the bushes and pulled a confused and barely conscious Billy Zirkel out of the snow-covered greenery.

"Billy? Are you OK?" Charlotte called out.

"The limo. Where is it?" Billy's speech was groggy. If Charlotte didn't know him better, she might think that Billy had been nipping on a bottle as the brief wedding ceremony was conducted.

"You don't know?" Don Dunkel called out over Brenda's shoulder. "You were driving it."

13

"A couple of big guys jumped me. Next thing I knew, I was in the bushes, and I blacked out. Where did all of this snow come from? And where's the limo?"

Anyone in the wedding party could have told Billy the snow came down from the sky, but not a single one of them could tell him where the limousine was.

* * * *

"Well, this is starting off well," Chance Diamond said dryly. "It would appear that the limousine has been stolen."

"That would be stating the obvious," Charlotte answered her brother, equally dryly. They'd had this routine going all their lives. Charlotte had thought that Brenda would find it off-putting, but, like so many things in their life, she took it calmly. The pithy exchanges the sister and brother indulged in just made Brenda smile and give a little laugh. They made Marilyn roll her eyes in mock disgust, but both Chance and Charlotte could tell that she enjoyed a limited amount of family banter too.

"I must say that life isn't this exciting in Williamsburg," Chance countered.

"Which no doubt is the only reason you accepted the invitation to be here," Charlotte tossed back.

"Not true," Chance said, turning seriously. "We wouldn't have missed this moment for the world, Charlotte."

There was a brief moment of a sister, taken off guard, realizing just how great a brother she had and giving Chance a teary-eyed smile.

"How will we get to the reception?" Marilyn Diamond asked, evaporating the moment.

"I don't see much chance of that," Brenda said. "It's more a question whether the roads will be clear enough tomorrow to get us to the ship."

"I'm not even sure how we'll manage the two blocks home, as fast and heavy as this is falling," Charlotte interjected. "This doesn't look like it's going to let up for the rest of the day."

The only ones who looked even slightly happy were Sam and Rocket. They were tugging at the leashes Bea Helgerson held, wanting to go out and play in the snow.

"I'll see what I can do about transportation," Billy said. "There are a few cars at the station waiting to be picked up from servicing." He was groggy from the blow to his head, though, and wasn't steady on his feet yet.

"You are going straight home and staying there, Billy," Charlotte said. "You're in no condition to be driving anywhere. We'll manage. Do you think you can get home by yourself?"

"Yes, ma'am. I'm staying just up the street in the rooms behind the garage."

"Well, go there before it gets any worse out here. And if you're still groggy in the morning, call Doctor Stanton. And don't worry about us. In fact, call Doctor Stanton and have him check you out anyway."

"I'm sorry about this."

"It's not your fault. We're just sorry you got mugged in the process. I'll call the sheriff's office when we get home. When they can get here, no doubt they'll need a statement from you—and they'll help you clear this with the limousine service."

"Right then," Tony Trice said. And as they watched Billy Zirkel struggle away in the snow, Tony clicked his cell phone shut and took charge. "I managed to get through to the reception and told them to have a good time without us. God only knows when or if any of them will get home tonight. I'll trudge on up to the house and see if I can get Charlotte's Escape back here—Neither Brenda's Jaguar roadster nor my Maserati will be much use in this stuff."

"I'll pull out the Buick instead," Don Dunkel broke in. "It should be OK for a couple of trips to Brenda and Charlotte's house. But I fear it might not be able to get you all to the Baltimore pier tomorrow."

"That's the least of our worries at the moment, Don," Brenda said. "Don't even think of trying. I doubt that many, if any, of the passengers will be making it to the Baltimore pier tomorrow if this keeps up."

"What about the photos at the reception?" This asked by Walt Miller, the volunteer photographer.

"There are cameras on the tables at the reception," Brenda answered. "They'll just have to photograph themselves."

"OK," Walt answered in a relieved voice.

"We'll see about getting you home," Tony said, turning to Walt.

"Oh, don't bother with me. I'll just cut through the Baptist church parking lot and go over onto Main Street. I'll get covered with snow either way, but I can just take a hot bath when I get home."

"Yes, if the power . . ." Charlotte was going to say "if the power holds," but just then the exterior floodlights on the church went out. There was still a glow from inside, though, where candles were burning and their light was reflecting off the stained-glass windows. Otherwise, the power appeared to have gone off all over the village. She turned to say something to Walt, but he'd already struck out in the snow.

When Charlotte turned back, she saw Brenda retreating into the church proper. Don Dunkel had already gone back up the aisle. The church was connected with the rectory and the garage was accessible from inside that, so, if Dunkel could get his big black Buick out of the garage, he wouldn't have to plow through snow on foot.

Brenda had sunk down in one of the back pews, and Sam and Rocket were both there with her, nuzzling their muzzles into her lap.

"I'm so sorry, Brenda," Charlotte said as she sat down in the pew in front of where Brenda was sitting and turned to her. "This is starting out to be a horrid honeymoon. I don't want you to cry on our wedding day."

Brenda was smiling when she looked up, though, and gave one of her signature laughs that thrilled so many movie goers. "Nonsense, Charlotte. We can honeymoon anywhere, just as long as we're together. This will give us some memorable stories to tell, I'm sure. And you said all along that you wanted a quiet wedding."

"I didn't say I wanted snow, though. Ah, I see the headlights of a car at the front of the church. Don managed to get his Buick around. Shall we?"

"Let's let Bea go ahead, and the rest. Let's sit here with Sam and Rocket for a few minutes and savor this moment. Just our nuclear family. Isn't the church lovely in full candlelight?"

"You always manage to see the best in everything," Charlotte said. She heaved herself up and went out to the narthex and told the others to go on ahead. Then she came back and sat in the pew next to Brenda and the two cuddled, with the two dogs laying their heads in laps—Sam in Charlotte's and Rocket in Brenda's. Months later, when Charlotte thought back on the events of their honeymoon, she was to remark on these moments as being the best of the first ten days of their marriage.

* * * *

As Don Dunkel, back from his first shuttle mission to take Brenda and Charlotte home on a second go at it, nosed his Buick gingerly through the drifting snow around the corner of Penn Street, where the Episcopal church was located, right onto River Street, where Brenda and Charlotte's house sat across the street on the left, the evening sky was lit up by a pulsating red light reflecting off the thickly falling snow flakes. When the car rounded the curve, they could see that this was caused by the red lights atop two sheriff's department cars parked at haphazard angles in front of the Hopewell House Inn B&B owned by Joyce and Todd Vale. The B&B was located directly across River Street from Brenda and Charlotte's house.

Joyce was a native of the village and this had been her family home. She'd grown up with Brenda, but both had left for many years—Brenda to Hollywood and Joyce to New York to work as a mainstream publishing house editor. She'd met Todd, working in international insurance, in New York, and they had returned to Hopewell in retirement to open the B&B.

The Vales had been invited to the wedding reception but hadn't gone. Their excuse was that they had guests in the B&B to take care of, but Charlotte suspected that Joyce still blamed her for having caused the arrest of Joyce's daughter for theft in the village and for the eventual murder of the daughter for having seen something she shouldn't have. Relations had been strained the last three years between those in the two large houses, one a federal manse and the other a rambling Victorian gingerbread house, across the street from each other. Charlotte's difficulty was with Joyce, not her husband, however. Todd, who was the town's vice mayor to Charlotte's position as mayor, would have gone to the reception, Charlotte was confident, if it had been up to him—but it wasn't. Joyce was a strong-willed woman, which also helped explain why she didn't get on so well with Charlotte, another strong-willed woman.

The inn was lit up by candlelight in the downstairs and in one of the rooms over the inn's parlor. Charlotte could make out movement of human figures in both that room and downstairs.

"What's going on over there?" Brenda asked. "Were the police cars there when you ferried the others to the house, Don?"

"No. They must have just arrived. Here we are at your curb, though. I'm afraid this is as close as I can get you to the house."

"Thanks, Don. You're a gem," Brenda said, as she looked at the piles of snow she'd have to go through to get to the house. The front door of the first story above an English basement opened, and Tony was there with a bundle of coats and boots, including Brenda's trusty Wellington boots, and was coming down the steps from the front porch and wading through the snow toward the Buick before Brenda could get her car door open.

"Speaking of gems, your son appears to be coming to the rescue," Dunkel said. "You ladies stay in the car until Tony gets here and then bundle up real well for getting up to the house."

Charlotte hadn't said a word since they turned the corner.

"When you're bundled up, go over to the Vale's, Charlotte," Brenda said. "I know you want to."

"We're off on our honeymoon if we can get there," Charlotte answered. "I can't get entangled in another mystery of any sort. It wouldn't be fair."

"I don't expect you to change, Charlotte. Crime and mystery ferret you out. I don't want you wondering what that's all about. You go on now. You're the town's mayor; you have a right to know why the sheriff is here on business on a snowy night. It looks very much like we won't be able to get to the ship tomorrow anyway and that we'll be honeymooning right here. We'll have our loved ones around us and that's all that matters. You go on over there now. I'm as curious as you are about what's wrong. Joyce may be in a snit with us, but she's a childhood friend and I care about her."

When Tony reached them and the car door opened, Sam and Rocket burst out of the car and into the snow to play, neatly eluding Tony's attempts to keep the dogs from getting loose while he handed over the coats and boots.

The two women bundled up as best they could and awkwardly stumbled out of the car into snow that came up above the bottom of the car doors. Brenda headed toward the house and Charlotte toward the B&B, while Pastor Dunkel spun the wheels of the Buick, getting it turned around in the driveway and eventually managing to creep back up Penn Street toward the rectory. The last thing he'd said was that he regretted that he didn't think he could drive the wedding party into Baltimore the next day—even if the Buick had had room for the entire wedding party. Both Brenda and Charlotte brushed that off and expressed their gratitude once again that he had conducted the service and then gotten them back home.

As Charlotte struggled toward the porch of the Hopewell Inn, she noticed that there was a car that had slipped off the road and into a tree at the northern side of the inn. It very much looked like Grady Tarbell's Subaru Outback. Grady, a resident of the village, lived on the next street up from Penn Street, on the Spring Street extension of the two-block Main Street business section. He lived here but he worked as a professor at Washington College in Chesterton, Maryland, a good distance to the north of the village, beyond Easton.

Todd answered Charlotte's knock on the B&B door and let her in.

"Is everything all right over here?" Charlotte asked. "Is that Grady's car against that tree? Is he—?"

"Everyone's not really OK," Todd answered. "But Grady's fine. It's no one from the village. There's been a death of a guest—and two others are missing."

"A death?" Charlotte asked.

But she no sooner said that then a voice floating down from the staircase bellowed, "I should have known you'd be here johnny on the spot."

Charlotte recognized the voice and greeted the Talbot County sheriff, Haws Wainwright, as he descended the stairs. Behind him was the deputy assigned to the Hopewell area, David Burch. Burch, who had worked well with Charlotte in the past, gave Charlotte a welcoming smile. Wainwright, who had had his hands slapped when Charlotte implicated him in taking a few bribes and whose investigations more often than not were upstaged by Charlotte's more nimble ability to solve crimes than his, wasn't nearly as welcoming.

"We came from Don Dunkel's church," Charlotte said. "We couldn't miss your cars with the red lights going. I don't want to get involved with whatever this is—Brenda and I are leaving on a cruise tomorrow—but we're neighbors, so naturally we wonder what it is."

"Murder is what it is," Wainwright said. "There's a dead guy up there in one of the bedrooms. Shot between the eyes. He's a foreigner. A Russian, we think, from his ID. Some sort of embassy attaché."

"Oh, I saw a car off the road by the inn that looked like Grady Tarbell's. I thought—"

"It is mine," Grady said. He appeared in the parlor door into the front hall. Joyce Todd came into view beside him. She wasn't looking any too happy. Charlotte could understand why she wouldn't be happy even without a dead body in one of her best guestrooms, because having Grady here would be an embarrassment to her. That daughter Charlotte had caused to be arrested had been born to Joyce out of wedlock—and she had been Grady's daughter. Grady had grown up in the village with Joyce and Brenda and had fooled around when they were seniors in high school. But he and Joyce had hardly spoken to each other since she had returned to Hopewell married to Todd. Todd knew

20

of the relationship Joyce and Grady had once had, but he seemed to accept that they had just been kids at the time and that it no longer meant anything. It was Joyce who stewed about the issue and avoided any mention of it.

"I only made it home from Chesterton this far in the snow when the car slid off the road," Grady said. "I could have walked home, but the Vales invited me to have dinner here first."

"So the police didn't come because you were wrecked?" Charlotte asked.

"No, we came because there's a dead man in the front bedroom upstairs. And two other men, companions of his, missing," Wainwright said. "All of them Russian, we think. They came in earlier this afternoon, checked into the B&B."

"They had us wondering, though," Todd Vale added. "They didn't appear to be tourists of any sort. They wore suits and spoke with heavy accents. And we don't get much business in March. It's not a good month for us. Joyce and I were out back trying to clear snow off the parking lot when the man was killed. We didn't even hear the shot as muffled up as we were."

"March is the cruelest month," Charlotte murmured, but no one seemed to have heard her.

"When the men didn't come down for dinner, Todd went up and checked on them," Joyce said, coming into the conversation for the first time. "He found only one of the men and he was dead. Thank god it wasn't me who found the body," she added. "We called the sheriff straightaway."

"I came from your reception," David Burch said. "Everyone there seems to be having a good time. I'm sorry that you and Ms. Boynton—"

Wainwright, who hadn't been invited to the reception, broke in, "So that's what's here. I hope you don't plan on—"

"No, certainly not," Charlotte said. "I'll leave you to it. If we can get off tomorrow, we're leaving from Baltimore on a seven-day cruise to the Bahamas. Just wanted some sort of idea what was happening here. Being the town mayor and all."

Charlotte was backing toward the door, and no one but David Burch looked the least bit unhappy about that.

"Oh, but one thing before I leave," Charlotte said as she reached the door. "You said two men were missing. Is the car the three came in missing too?"

"No," Joyce answered. "They came in a big, black SUV. It's parked in the back parking lot—so snowed in it's not moving until we shovel it out. Todd and I had to shovel around it to get a clear path to the street. I just looked and it's still there."

"Then I may have another piece of the puzzle to throw into the mix," Charlotte said.

"I doubt this could get any more mixed up than it is already," Wainwright answered.

"We were going to call you in the morning anyway, Sheriff. Don Dunkel had to drive the wedding party back to Brenda's house from the church because two men mugged Billy Zirkel. He was to drive us to Easton in a limousine—and they stole the limousine. Might be your two missing men. Maybe they wanted to leave in a hurry, saw that they couldn't get their SUV out, and took the limousine. It might mean they are gone now, out of Hopewell."

She opened the door and was half way through it, when Wainwright called out. "Just a minute. I'll need a statement on that—on the stolen limo."

"Billy Zirkel is the one who was mugged, and he leased the limousine for us. You should get your statement from him. You don't want me to become involved in this, you said."

Wainwright was huffing but hadn't thought what to say when Charlotte got out on the porch. David Burch followed her out of the door.

"If you'll e-mail me from the ship when you can, Ms. Diamond, I'll give you status reports on how this unfolds. I know you'll want to know, and I'll bet you can help us unravel it."

"Thanks, David," Charlotte answered him in a low voice. "It certainly does sound intriguing. We'll see about me asking about it, though. And we may not be going anywhere tomorrow. We needed the limo to get everyone to the pier. And with this snow—"

"How many have to go?" Deputy Burch asked.

"There are six in the party," Charlotte answered.

"I'll have two police cars with four-wheel drive here at 8:00 a.m. tomorrow, Ms. Diamond. We'll get you all to that ship on time."

"You don't have to do that, Dave," Charlotte said.

"For all the cases you've helped me with, it will be an honor to do it," he answered.

"Won't Sheriff Wainwright—?"

"When I tell him it will get you on that ship and out of Hopewell while he investigates this—or tries to—I'm sure he'll be glad to help provide the transportation. It should be my day off tomorrow anyway, and one of the other deputies will be off too and I'm sure will be happy to drive. We won't tell the sheriff about the e-mail contact, but I'm sure we'll need your expertise sooner or later. It's a strange case. Someone from the Russian embassy murdered here in Hopewell. Who would have thought?"

The both laughed. "I see your point," Charlotte said. "8:00 a.m. it is, then. And thanks, Dave."

By the time Charlotte reached the house, Bea and the men had gotten all of the fireplaces going and the house was toasty and lovely with all of its rich fabrics and Sheraton and Chippendale antique furniture bathed in the warm glow of candlelight. We are lucky, Charlotte thought, to have a vintage home with a fireplace in nearly every room—and not just fireplaces, but also fireplaces that still work.

She found everyone, including both dogs, who Bea had corralled and gotten dried off and fluffed up, in the more modern family room behind the kitchen, which, thankfully, had a fireplace with a roaring fire going. All except the dogs were drinking hot toddies and seemed to be quite cozy.

"Honeymooning here won't be so bad," Brenda said after Charlotte had reported on why the sheriff department cruisers were across the street. "We can manage nicely right here."

"Don't unpack," Charlotte said. "Dave Burch is bringing two four-wheel-drive vehicles tomorrow at 8:00 to get us to the ship. Then we can leave all of this nonsense behind."

"I'm sure it isn't that simple," Brenda said with a twinkle in her eye. "Dave promised to keep you posted on the mystery at the inn, didn't he? You wouldn't be leaving this mystery so easily otherwise."

"Yes, he did," Charlotte said sheepishly. "But I haven't promised to ask him what's happening."

"But you will," Brenda said. "I know you can't resist. And I'll want to know too. Our cruise won't be complete without a little mystery going."

Smiling, and full of contentment and joy at the more deeply committed relationship she was embarking on with Brenda, Charlotte pulled Brenda to her on the sofa facing the fireplace and kissed her on the temple. The two sighed in unison, as did two other cuddling couples. Even Sam and Rocket were huddled together and seemed to be sighing. Only Bea was quietly bustling around in the kitchen, figuring out what she could fix for a supper for this crowd—and this was when she was at her happiest. It would be a feast. Everyone was so happy with the present circumstances that no one shouted "Hallelujah" when the power came back on—and no one bothered to turn on the lights. The candlelight and light from the fireplace suited their moods just fine.

Little did Brenda know, though, just how many mysteries their cruise would entail—and not little ones, either. And certainly not pleasant ones.

Chapter Two: Day One; The Baltimore Cruise Line Pier

"We made it," Marilyn Diamond said as they reached the back of a long, winding line of travelers waiting to feed into passport control and immigration at the Baltimore pier. All of them were struggling with a carry-on or two plus the bulky winter clothes they were bundled in. This was in stark contrast to the sunny beaches they hoped to find in the Caribbean within just a couple of days.

"We made it thanks to David Burch and his friend with the two four-wheel-drive SUVs," Brenda said.

"What's really surprising is that many others made it here in the snow as well," Chance Diamond remarked.

They'd had a grueling drive around Route 50 and into Baltimore in continuing snow that turned into icy rain as they got closer to the port. Every two miles or so Charlotte would declare that even if they made it to the ship, not enough passengers would do so for the ship to bother to sail. In response, Brenda would just sigh, point out that David Burch was expertly mastering the conditions of the road, and bury herself deeper in the warm overcoat she was wearing.

But each time Charlotte suggested that they just turn around and try to make it back to Hopewell, declaring that those in the other car with the other deputy, Charlotte's brother and sister-in-law, and Tony's girlfriend, were probably cursing them out for not turning back, David Burch would point out that the roads were progressively getting better as the temperatures warmed and more vehicles ventured out. And sure enough, when they reached the parking lot for the cruise, there was a long, double line of cars waiting to discharge their luggage before joining another long, four-vehicle-wide line waiting to pay to park. Then Charlotte changed her tune into noting that perhaps they were the last ones who had made it to the dockside.

"Never underestimate a winter-weary American's determination to reach the sunny Caribbean, especially under bad-weather conditions at home," Tony quipped as they all settled back for the long wait to relinquish their luggage. After they had done so and the two police cars had dispensed the travelers and their carry-on luggage outside the terminal and driven away, Tony also remarked on how lucky they were not to have to wait to pay to park too.

Marilyn Diamond, Chance's wife, seconded that, saying that all of the passengers must have arrived at the same time and that they were lucky that they had bypassed that second wait. Her husband just gave her a horse laugh, though, as he opened the door to the terminal for them to enter. He merely pointed inside, where a long line of bundled-up travelers snaked back and forth in a not-so-small space, waiting for passport control and a turn to go through the same security checks they have in airports.

"Oh, my," Marilyn said, with a sigh, to which Charlotte added, "Look beyond the security check frames. That's not a mirror back there; that's another line of people waiting to go through security as well from the other side."

As the occasion would have it—everyone having stories to share of the grueling trip to get to the ship on time through the snow, sleet, and ice—most of those in line were both congenial and talkative. Some were almost giddy in relief to have made it to the pier before the ship sailed.

Tony's tennis pro girlfriend, Michelle, bent down to converse with a young girl holding tightly to a man's hand and looking bewildered and awestruck all at the same time. The girl's eyes lit up and she could be seen to visibly relax as Michelle talked with her. Michelle had the disarming touch.

"Isn't she cute?" Marilyn whispered to a somewhat disgruntled Charlotte, who was pawing through her carry-on bag in search of her elusive passport that somehow had slipped from where Charlotte had conveniently stashed it so that she wouldn't have to do exactly what she was doing—pawing through her carry-on in a slow-shuffling line.

Charlotte grunted her assent as her hand closed over what might be her passport but turned out to be one of the paperbacks she had brought instead.

"She appears only to be with that young man," Marilyn continued. "No mother evident. I wonder if he's widowed or divorced and taking his daughter on a cruise in what custody time he is permitted."

"You have the sensitivities of a writer, Marilyn," Charlotte said. "You start weaving stories about any people who catch your fancy."

"It's not me consciously weaving the stories, Charlotte," Marilyn responded. "It's my mind that is engaged with snippets of this and that it sees and does the weaving for me, dropping the results into my lap when and as it likes. And it's because I am a minister, I think. I must always be aware of trying circumstances that pull at people—to see people who need help or a steadying hand."

"Then that's something ministers must share with writers," Charlotte said. "But with different purposes. You are called to minister to them, while writers are motivated to pull interesting stories from them. But you may well be right that he's taking a daughter on a dream vacation. But it's March. And there seem to be quite a few children in this line. I wouldn't have thought—"

"It's the week between Palm Sunday and Easter," Brenda chimed in. "This must be some sort of school spring break."

"Terrific," Charlotte muttered. "I didn't think about that. But if I'd known—"

Her sentence was cut short by a Customs official calling out over the hubbub. "Have passports and a form of photo ID out and ready to show, ladies and gentlemen, please. And no liquids beyond this point."

All adults in line around them started fishing out documentation from wherever they'd tucked it, while simultaneously trying to respond to the children hanging on their arms and excitedly asking question about what certainly was a new experience for most of them. Charlotte's hand found her own passport and the wallet with her photo ID driver's license in it— right where she had put them earlier in the morning for convenient access and right where she had looked for them several times after they'd reached the terminal without finding them. With a sigh of "Why does that always happen?" she extracted the documents.

She looked up, startled, and at full attention. Her training as an FBI agent had clicked in, and she had no idea why. She let her eyes scan the close-packed coiled lines around her. Something in the crowd had piqued her interest—or, more precisely, her guard—in her subconscious. What was it? Was it anything at all? She was some years retired now and her investigative abilities were atrophying, she feared. But there had been something in the crowd.

Her eyes scanned over an elderly and thin man of distinguished bearing. But her attention moved on. He wasn't the type to evoke what she thought of as her "crime" instinct.

Then she saw it—rather, she saw them both. The one irritated her but she saw no threat in it. The other one in conjunction with the first, though. . . .It was seeing separate groups of rather grim-looking Hispanic young men, all cut from the same cloth—dressed in jeans and T-shirts and leather jackets almost to a man and looking more wary and slightly nervous than one would expect those embarking on a Caribbean ship cruise would look. But what was arresting was that, although they were scattered in the line in groups of two or three, there seemed to be a visual connection being maintained between the men—like they were all together in one group. Why, she thought, didn't they come across as vacationers? And why were they scattered through the line like they didn't want to be seen together as a group? Were they, in fact, an innocuous party and were just separated in line because they had arrived at the port, and at the end of the line, separately?

And were they really scattered at all? Several were on cell phones, and it seemed like they were talking with each other, across the departure hall.

The passport women put a stop to that, though, by calling out, quite possibly just because this was the set time she did so rather than because she had seen anything amiss, "Passports at the ready, please, when you reach the top of the line, ladies and gentlemen. And no liquids beyond this point, please—and please turn off all cell phones. No cell phone use in the terminal, please. Not again until you reach the ship."

Charlotte quickly looked from group to group of young, Hispanic men, and although they scowled and some seemed to need to have the announcement translated to them, they all did put their devices away. Then they all looked around them with guilty expressions on their faces—at least they looked like guilty expressions to Charlotte's trained eyes.

Was she just weaving stories like Marilyn was prone to do on the basis of just a glance? Or were Charlotte's investigator antenna still in working order? Maybe it wasn't only ministers and writers who were prone to projecting life stories and hidden motivations from brief observations of the people around them. Maybe this was an instinct connected with criminal investigation too. Whatever it was, Charlotte knew she wouldn't be able to keep herself from observing what the young men were doing whenever and wherever she saw them during the cruise. It was surprising, but she thought there would be no difficulty in separating them out from the rest of those on the cruise even if they subsequently dressed more in keeping with the trip.

The other thing Charlotte noticed was something that she noticed nearly all of the time when she and Brenda were out in public beyond the confines of Hopewell. Although people were mostly absorbed with their own excitement and impatience to be getting on board—and talking of the difficulty of getting to the pier in the snow and icy rain—within their own travel party or with those in proximity to them in line, they also were giving some attention to looking at Brenda. As often was the case, there was curiosity and perplexity in the gazes they sent Brenda's way, most of them not openly staring, but looking guardedly at her and, some of them, whispering to their travel companions. People were half recognizing Brenda, but since the Brenda Boynton Charlotte and her companions knew was out of the context here of being the celebrated movie star, Brenda Brandon, few of the travelers tagged her as more than a lookalike, although they kept returning their eyes to her and speculating.

"I think you're being recognized," Charlotte whispered to Brenda. "I told you this might happen if we honeymooned so close to the States. I fear that by halfway into the cruise you'll be pestered right and left for autographs."

"Oh, I don't think I'm as well-known as that," Brenda said, flashing Charlotte one of her radiant signature screen smiles.

Charlotte fancied she heard a gasp of recognition from more than one quarter in the line. "Oh, I think you are," she said. "And stop smiling; it's a dead giveaway."

"I can't smile on the whole cruise?" Brenda asked with an amused lilt in her voice. She tilted her head slightly in another of her signature moves, and Charlotte detected a few more gasps.

"Only in our cabin. And I plan to keep you in there to myself much of the cruise."

"It's a good thing we got a large cabin then," Brenda said with a little laugh—which made Charlotte grab her arm.

"Stop that too. You're doing the whole Brenda Brandon performance."

"Yes, ma'am," Brenda said.

Mercifully, they had reached the front of the line and Charlotte had discovered she'd let her passport and driver's license sink into the interior of her open carry-on again. Thus her attention was turned to diving for them again in panic as the passport control officer put out a hand to examine the documents.

Charlotte thought the worst of the crowding was over when they got through the line waiting for passport control and then the security check, but when they got beyond this point they found themselves in a vast hall, teeming with travelers in a long line leading up to the cruise check-in desks. Charlotte saw what must have been fifteen or sixteen desks serving yet another snaking line three or four times longer than the one they'd just been through. Before the line started there was a cruise line official checking the Internet printouts of the sea passes of the passengers.

When she handed the one for Brenda and her to the official, the woman smiled broadly and said, "Please proceed around to the right to the priority line."

A feeling of tightness gripped Charlotte momentarily with the thought that the cruise line had already ferreted out Brenda's real identity and that they'd be the subject of far more unctuous attention from the beginning of the cruise than they had wanted. Brenda must have seen and deciphered what was behind that look, though, as she leaned over and said, "I'm sure it's because we have a suite."

And indeed that was the reason, because both the Diamonds and Tony and Michelle, who had top-deck junior suites stringing down from Charlotte and Brenda's larger suite, also were directed to the priority line.

Must calm down, Charlotte chided herself. We're on vacation—on our honeymoon. I must stop scrutinizing everyone and everything. I promised Brenda I would just lay back for the week. Even as she thought this, though, her mind went back to the murdered Russian in the Vales' B&B across from their house in Hopewell and to speculating on what that meant.

"What?" she said, looking up at the cruise reception desk woman who had asked her for something as they reached the front of the short priority line.

"Our sea pass printout, Charlotte," Brenda said. "You look like you have a death grip on it."

"Oh, this," Charlotte said.

She handed the sea pass to the woman and then thought she noted a slight wavering of the woman's smile as she looked at it. Something wrong? The sea pass not in order? Charlotte's mind raced. She jabbed the tips of her fingernails into her palms and cried out inside herself just to relax.

The woman at the desk excused herself and left for a few minutes. Had she done that for the people in line ahead of them, Charlotte wondered. She hadn't noticed. She should have been more observant. But then the woman was back, showing a bit of a nervous smile, and was handing them their plastic ID cards that were to be used for just about everything on the cruise needed to show identity or pay for anything, and they were receiving instructions on the next step of the boarding and a few basic preliminary bits of information on the start of the cruise.

They were directed to walk across the fronts of all the other desks, with the snaking line of those whose wait would be much longer to their left and then to a larger waiting room, where people were waiting for their turn to be able to walk aboard the ship at last. At the entrance of this area was yet another smiling woman in the cruise line uniform, directing people where to sit with a group waiting to board. Standing beside her was an unsmiling man in a dark suit.

As the party approached, the man said, "Charlotte Diamond? Is Charlotte Diamond in your group?"

"Yes, that's me," Charlotte answered, pulling aside from her party.

"Could you come with me, please, Ms. Diamond? You can join your party before the sailing, but your presence is required elsewhere briefly."

"We'll wait for you here in this waiting room," Brenda said.

"That won't be necessary," the smiling cruise hostess said, looking at their sea passes. "You are in suites. You can proceed directly on board. Your party will join you later."

"It's just a formality," the man said. "Ms. Diamond will be with you shortly."

Not convinced by the smiles and giving Brenda a quizzical look but then smiling herself in assurance when she saw Brenda starting to become distressed, Charlotte followed the man back to the area of the check-in desks, but this time walking behind them. She felt a little numb. All this time she'd been worried about Brenda attracting attention, and now all of those people in that long, snaking line, were watching her being escorted to who knows where for what possible purpose.

Charlotte couldn't think of anything she'd been guilty of. So why, she wondered, did she feel like she'd been guilty of something? So far this honeymoon had been a real bummer.

If anything, she thought, she had been too tuned in to looking for the guilt in others. She hadn't been as tuned in as she thought she had been, though, because she hadn't given a second glance to the distinguished looking older man who had been quite jolly in the jostling line snaking its way around to get through passport control and who, every once in a while, got a hand into a purse or carry-on bag or pocket of one or another distracted passenger and came out with something precious. If she'd been more attentive to him, she would have worried about how closely he had followed Brenda and the others as they were moving to the ship after Charlotte had been separated from them.

Chapter Three: Even Before the Ship Sails

"Hello, Charlotte. Sorry to pull you off line, but I wanted to consult with you about something."

"Brian? Brian Harden? What . . . ?" Charlotte couldn't think of what "what" to ask Harden about. She hadn't seen him since they had retired within a month of each other from the Annapolis FBI office. Brian had been a good agent, if not an outstanding one. Somewhat of a plodder, but he'd frequently come to her for advice, and although she'd always had the feeling he thought women had no place in the FBI, he had never blown off what she had to say. She vaguely remembered when he'd quietly left the service at the first opportunity.

"I'm head of security for the cruise lines sailing out of Baltimore port now. It's usually a sleeper of a job with good pay for a government retiree, but yesterday and today haven't been the best."

"You're telling me," Charlotte said.

"Had a hard time getting here in the snow?" Harden asked.

"Yes. And that's the least of it. I got married yesterday and everything since then has been downhill."

"Congratulations on that. I didn't know you'd gotten married again. But I did see your name on the manifest and hoped I'd be able to see you—and, as it turned out, to consult with you. I had hoped to be able to greet you under better circumstances, though."

"What's wrong with the circumstances?"

"We're keeping it as much hush-hush as we can, but there was a suspicious death on board on the previous cruise. Just yesterday or the night before, it appears. One of the women guests. The Baltimore police are working the case, but I have to see what I can do too. It's a dicey matter because it happened somewhere out in the Chesapeake Bay channel. Not exactly squarely in the Baltimore police's jurisdiction. The cruise line sees it as my problem, and, of course, it would be a publicity nightmare if the press made a big splash with it. I feel a bit isolated in these instances. I'd appreciate the opportunity to run it past you and see what you think. Also, we have a room attendant who seems to have more to say then she's willing to tell me. I thought perhaps if another woman—"

"Yes, certainly I'll help. Just get me on the ship in time." At least he knew he had trouble relating to women, Charlotte thought. She'd encountered many in the FBI who didn't realize that about themselves.

"I'll do that even if I have to send you down the Chesapeake after the ship in a pilot boat," Harden said, the relief evident in his voice.

Just then a young man knocked on the door to Harden's office and called him away momentarily. Charlotte took the opportunity to stand and walk around the office. She was drawn, by habit, to a wall of wanted posters, looking for wanted criminals she may have encountered before. Her eyes zeroed in on one poster and she nearly gasped with surprise. She was still closely reading it when Harden reappeared. She was on the brink of saying something to him when he launched right into the case on his plate.

"The victim is a woman in her early forties. An older husband—by maybe fifteen years or so. She was found stabbed in their cabin on deck seven, a balcony room. Her husband was found hunched in a chair in the room, covered in blood—both hers and his."

"His too?"

"Yep, he'd been stabbed too. He's been hauled off to the hospital in shock, they say. And the Baltimore police haven't been able to get anything out of him. The door to the balcony was open and it was frigid in the cabin—as you can imagine. You know what yesterday and today have been like here in Baltimore."

"So, the thinking is that he did it?"

"At the moment, yes. It's almost always the spouse. Some of the attendants said they'd been hearing the two arguing in the passageways the last couple of days. The dining room attendant said by the end of the cruise only the husband was showing up for dinner. A couple of the bar attendants said the wife drank her supper in various on-board bars. And she spent much of her time there. So, the Baltimore police are running with the idea that it was a clear-cut domestic incident. But I'm not so sure."

"Why not?"

"For one thing, the knife was recovered. It was one of those fancy engraved ones that had been bought in Nassau. It had touristy Nassau markings on it."

"And there's a problem with that—that it was from Nassau? The cruise docked in Nassau didn't it?"

"According to the ship's departure and return records, neither of them got off in Nassau or at either of the other two stops. If the knife belonged to one of them, they must have either brought it on board with them in Baltimore or gotten it from another passenger who got off in Nassau."

"Yes, I see that as a wrinkle. The possibility of a third party having been involved."

"The Baltimore police don't seem to be worried about it. But there's something else. Their cabin attendant, a Filipina named Analiza Quatro, spoke of the two having spats, but I think she knows more than that. I can't get her to open up. But I thought maybe you could . . ."

"I'll be happy to talk with her. Is she here?"

"She's on her way down from the ship. That's what I went off to ask for just now—for her to be brought here. Thanks for doing this, Charlotte. I just have a bad feeling about this one."

"That's what we were trained to do, Brian—to follow up on our instincts, whatever they were. I'd be happy to talk to the woman. Perhaps, in turn, you could do something for me."

"Yes, of course. If it's something I can do."

"That wanted poster up there—the third one in from the left on the top row—could you see if you can find out more about the circumstances of that case and get the information to me on board?"

"You recognize someone?"

"Maybe. I'm not sure. And I wouldn't want to say more without being sure."

"Yes, I can do that. Ah, here she is now." There had been a knock on the door, and a short woman in a cruise line attendant's uniform and looking wary and a bit frightened was escorted into the room.

"Thank you for coming, Analiza. This is a friend of mine, Ms. Diamond. She'll be on your next cruise, and I've asked her to speak with you. She's a good person. You can trust her. Here, have a seat over here. I'll leave you two alone."

Analiza perched on a chair like a bird ready to take off at the first opportunity.

"Relax, Analiza," Charlotte said. "It's just you and me here and I'm a passenger, not security. Would you like something to drink?"

"No, ma'am, thank you, ma'am."

"Analiza. Such a pretty name. Is it from someone else in your family?"

"Yes, ma'am. The name is popular in the Philippines, where I come from. It was my aunt's name. She died right before I was born, and my mother gave the name to me to keep her memory alive."

"What a wonderful thing to do. Is that a Philippine tradition? And, please, call me Charlotte."

"That's a pretty name too, ma'am. And, yes, it is a custom of my country."

Charlotte spent several minutes in such chat to give the young woman assurance and to build trust. It wasn't long before she could see the tension draining out of Analiza, which would allow for more probing questions.

"About the Abbots, Analiza. Were they a nice couple?"

"Well, *he* was, Mr. Abbot was, ma'am . . . Charlotte. But he seemed so sad. I don't think he was well."

Charlotte spent a minute clucking with Analiza about Mr. Abbot's health before she honed in again.

"You didn't mention whether Mrs. Abbot was nice too."

"All of our passengers are nice people, of course," Analiza said.

"But you thought Mr. Abbot was nicer than Mrs. Abbot, didn't you?"

Analiza pursed her lips. "Mrs. Abbot has passed; it's not good to speak of the dead badly."

"But Mr. Abbot may be in trouble over his wife's death. Do you think that is as it should be?"

Analiza thought on that for a moment. "We aren't supposed to speak badly of our guests. I could be in trouble."

"I'm not with the cruise line, Analiza. If there is something that should be known that would help Mr. Abbot, you can tell me. I promise that I wouldn't tell the cruise line anything that would get you in trouble. If you can help in finding out why Mrs. Abbot was killed, I think the cruise line would want you to do that. And I'll certainly tell them that you did so while remaining sensitive to the passengers' privacy to the extent you could. That's quite commendable of you. I'm sure the cruise line will appreciate your discretion."

"Thank you. Still, one doesn't speak ill of the dead."

"But there's something about Mrs. Abbot that made her not a nice person. Is that what you mean? Do you know something that would help the truth come out?"

"I did hear some of what they argued about. And my friend Natalia told me something too."

"Did they argue about Mrs. Abbot's drinking."

Analiza pursed her lips again and crossed her arms on her bosom. "Mrs. Abbot did drink a lot on board, yes. And that was some of what they argued about."

"And what your friend, Natalia, told you was something else too? Is Natalia a cabin attendant too?"

"Yes. I'm sure Mrs. Abbot wasn't in her right mind when she had a lot to drink. People do strange things on boat cruises, things they never would do in their own homes."

"I'm sure that's right, Analiza, that people are different when they are on a vacation like this. I'm sure that Mrs. Abbot was a different person normally. She went to another man's cabin? Is that what Natalia told you?"

"Yes, ma'am," Analiza answered in a quiet, faltering voice.

"Thank you, Analiza," Charlotte said, reaching over and patting the trembling woman on the knee. "I promise you won't be in any trouble for telling me this. You have been a great help, and this is something that needed to be told."

When Brian returned and Analiza was gone, Charlotte said. "I think your instincts are right, Brian. There is another attendant on board named Natalia. You might check into the men in the cabins she attended to. And also check these men with the ship's bar attendants to see if Mrs. Abbot was being cozy with any of them—and, if you can, check on whether that man left the ship in Nassau."

"Yes, I see your drift. We'll check that out. Thanks for your help. And I'll let you know how—and if—it all comes together."

"Is there anything else I can do?" Charlotte asked.

"Yes. I can't go on the cruise and the Baltimore police have finished with forensics on the cabin but asked us to seal it until the ship returns in case they want to take another look at it. When I told them you were on board, though, they asked if I could get you to look at the cabin too. Would you be willing to do that and to give us your assessment of the scene?"

"Sure, I could do that. Will you be there?"

"I can't sail with the ship. I work for all of the cruise lines departing from here, and there will be another ship arriving here tomorrow from a different line. There is a security crew on board your ship, though, and I've told the chief of security, Tim Kincaid, about you. If you'll check at the reception desk on board when you get on the ship, he's waiting to meet you. He'll give you a pass

40

card to the cabin. Thanks for doing this for us, Charlotte. I'll keep in touch via e-mail. Tim will get you hooked up with a free-use e-mail account. E-mailing from the ship is quite expensive. Feel free to use the account for all of your communication needs. It's the least we can do for you in return."

"No problem. I'll be happy to help in any way I can. And you'll let me know if there's more information on that wanted poster too?"

"Yes, certainly. But now I'm afraid we'll have to run to get you on the ship before they pull up the gangplank. This took longer than I expected."

"It's a regional thing, Brian. Someone like Analiza, who is from the Philippines, must be comfortable with you before opening up—especially if it entails doing something the cruise line cautions her not to do—breaking confidences on what the passengers say and do. I promised Analiza that she wouldn't be in trouble for what she told me. And if you want Natalia to reveal what she knows about Mrs. Abbot's activities, you'll need to make sure she has that assurance as well. They have been trained not to talk out of school nor to accuse without solid proof."

"I understand. I'll cover her."

Charlotte was a bit worried about Analiza and Natalia still, as the two obviously had been talking out of school about Sheila Abbot—at least to each other—but she was sure that Brian had gotten the message about what to pursue and what not to pursue if he wanted to get to the bottom of this mystery. She had given him quite a speech, but part of it was directed at herself, bolstering a decision she had made, right or wrong. She really should tell him what she suspected about the wanted poster she'd seen, but something Marilyn had said earlier had stuck in her mind, and she wanted to thoroughly check out what was what before proceeding—if she proceeded at all. From what she had observed, the situation might not be quite as the poster indicated.

But once again, she felt she was dropping into mysteries too often and too deeply. Why couldn't she just go on vacation and have a good time free of getting into anyone else's business or tragedies?

As they ran for the gangplank, another sour thought entered her mind. This murder on the ship was actually a godsend for her. Otherwise she would be having one humongous Internet bill while on this cruise in just keeping up with the mysteries she was already involved in. And then there was the time away from Brenda to deal with the communications. Perhaps she should pray for foul weather on the high seas between Baltimore and the Bahamas just to keep the e-mails at bay. But thinking about the possibility of that gave her no comfort either. This was shaping up to be one horrible honeymoon. And if she didn't make it to that gangplank that already looked like it was being drawn up, it couldn't possibly be a more miserable one, with Brenda in the sunny Bahamas and her in snowy Maryland.

Harden's commanding yell put a stop to the raising of the gangplank, though, and, in moments, Charlotte was safely aboard—or as safely as anyone else who was on board for this particular cruise.

Entering the ship and walking to the elevator hub, Charlotte got a nasty surprise. She encountered a group of other passengers bunched up in front of the elevators and looking up at the dials showing what decks the lifts were passing. All of them were passing by this deck—going both ways. Those waiting at the elevators weren't the least bit impressed, and Charlotte joined them in not being impressed.

One of the ship's crew members, who had been one of the attendants checking passengers in at the gangplank popped her head into the elevator lobby and chirped, "Sorry folks, the elevators have all been taken for getting the luggage up. They'll be free at 1:30. The stair hall is over there, just behind this bank of elevators."

"What deck are we on?" someone in the small, somewhat tense crowd asked.

"Deck two," the woman said and then she disappeared ahead of any jeers that might be sent her way.

Charlotte looked at her pass card. Deck eight, it said. Six flights of stairs. Her carry-on wasn't light and she'd already had to run to beat the gangplank raising. Brenda had noted that they'd need to be able to take special care to get their exercise on this cruise. Charlotte had hoped it wouldn't all come within the first half hour. She moved with the crowd into the stair hall and looked up at the daunting, open-tread stairs up to the next deck—enough of them that there was a landing at the half-way mark.

Six long flights of stairs to her deck and she was now standing on deck two. She had no idea what was on deck one and didn't really want to know either. She knew that decks two and three and half of deck four were the cheap seats—the relatively cheap cabins, she thought. Nothing on this cruise was cheap, of course. Half of the fourth deck was taken up with the lower level of the main dining room. The public decks were five and six, with the mezzanine level of the main dining room, the first level of the central atrium that went all the way up to a dome on the ninth deck, a casino and the first level of the Neptune theater on the fifth deck and the Seamaster main lounge, Brigantine bar, shopping mall, and mezzanine level of the Neptune theater on deck six. Deck seven was taken up with the balcony cabins, and deck eight, Charlotte's deck, included more of the balcony cabins and the junior suites and full suites. Charlotte and Brenda had a full suite and the others with them were in two nearby junior suites. Above them, on deck nine were the swimming pools, the Galleon free-seating café, and the health spa. The only thing above that deck were the mezzanine walking track around the swimming pool lined with lounge beds and the stairs up to the more intimate Mermaid lounge perched at the bow of the ship.

Gulping in several breaths and cinching up her belt, Charlotte plunged upward. When she had huffed up the intervening decks to the level of the suites, she found Brenda standing in the eighth-floor stair hall and talking with an elderly gentlemen. Brenda hadn't made it to their suite yet. As she stumbled on the last step up to deck eight, Charlotte also stumbled into yet another worry to have on the cruise.

"Oh, Charlotte, good. You made it," Brenda said cheerily. "As you can see I haven't made it to the cabin yet. I happened onto an old friend. You might recognize him. Glen Welden appeared in movies with me a good twenty years ago. Completely lost track of him. Glen, this is my Charlotte, Charlotte Diamond."

Despite the years, Glen was still quite the suave looker, tall and thin and as well dressed as a patrician, even if very casually. His backpack jangled a bit as he changed shoulders supporting it to shake hands with Charlotte, flashing her a brilliant smile. Not for the first time Charlotte wondered whether there were special acting classes for producing winning smiles on demand. If so, this Glen must have aced the course almost as well as Brenda had. He looked vaguely familiar to Charlotte, but she assumed, because Brenda had mentioned it, that she recognized him from the movies rather than from being the elderly gentleman her eyes had scanned across earlier in the terminal passport-control line.

"Charlotte and I are on our honeymoon. Charlotte's a retired senior FBI agent," Brenda said.

The handshake wavered just long enough for Charlotte to assume that Glen was put off by the knowledge that Brenda and she were married. Whether it was because he harbored a prejudice or, more likely, Charlotte thought, because of the obvious look of interest he had been giving Brenda when Charlotte huffed up the last section of stairs, it didn't really matter. The sudden weakness of the handshake told Charlotte that she needed to be wary of this man on this cruise.

Her instincts were spot on, but her assumptions weren't as sharp. It had been the identification of Charlotte as a retired FBI agent that had startled Welden and had caused him to go weak in the hand. It was the same revelation that caused him to shift the jangling backpack farther on his back, away from Charlotte. As he did so, it jangled again with the loot he had accumulated in the terminal waiting lines from several passengers who only now were beginning to discover that something of value was missing from their own carry-on luggage, purses, or pockets.

"We'll have to meet for drinks or something to update ourselves," Brenda was saying to Welden, who was nodding his head in agreement. She turned to Charlotte and looked at her expectantly.

"Yes, we certainly will," Charlotte responded on cue, trying to muster up a brilliant, all-act smile to seal an enthusiasm she didn't feel. She knew that her relationship with Brenda having been sealed by marriage should be enough assurance for her that

44

her fairytale life was real, but somehow it wasn't enough. Charlotte worried that it never would be enough—but she accepted that the worries were all hers, that Brenda had bent over backward to provide the assurances. Brenda was still a beautiful, charismatic woman. Charlotte knew she shouldn't expect men not to gravitate to her no matter what Brenda's feelings were. God knew Evan Worthington still gravitated to Charlotte in the same way. That too was a mystery to Charlotte, whose insecurities about her own appeal just wouldn't go away.

Chapter Four: Steaming Down the Chesapeake Bay

"Oh, lordy," Charlotte exclaimed as she was almost bowled over on the fifth deck landing—with three more to go—by a passel of excited, yodeling children racing down the stairs. Brenda had no more than gotten out introductions with her former movie colleague when Charlotte left the two on the eighth-deck landing and descended the stairs again because she had remembered that Brian Harden had asked her to stop at the ship's reception desk. She was to identify herself to Tim Kincaid, the ship's security chief, who Harden had told to accommodate Charlotte's communications needs and give her a pass card to the cabin where a murder had occurred. Her visit to Kincaid had not been a short one and the ship was under way before she ascended a second time to the eighth floor. She had used the stairs again, being in a hurry to be with Brenda again and the elevators now being clogged with passengers exploring the ship.

Why, oh why, didn't we check when school spring break was? she castigated herself, as she stopped on the seventh floor landing to catch her breath. She didn't want to be out of breath when she reached her suite on the next deck.

Brenda raced to the suite door when she heard Charlotte insert her sea pass card into the lock, and she came as close to knocking Charlotte over as the children on the stairs had.

If I'm going to be bowled over, this is the way I want it done, Charlotte thought. After giving Brenda a kiss and a hug in the corridor, not caring who saw them, Charlotte permitted herself to be dragged into the cabin. The two women weren't alone. There was a large sitting area in the suite and Chance and Marilyn Diamond and Tony Trice and Michelle Minor were all sitting around a coffee table, strawberry-colored drinks in hand in champagne glasses, and slathering crackers with cheese from a groaning board. Also, sitting in the middle of everything and looking slightly bewildered when he wasn't casting worshipping glances at Brenda was Glen Welden, the elderly actor friend of Brenda's. With a view to the looks he was giving Brenda, Charlotte hoped that he was as uncomfortable being there among chattering strangers as she was to have found him in the suite with her friends and family.

"Thank goodness you made the ship, Charlotte," Brenda said in a breathy voice. "I was afraid they'd dragged you off at Baltimore. Work again? Something about the Russian shot at Joyce's?"

"I'll tell you about it later," Charlotte murmured. "Nothing that important to us, and no, it's not about the shot Russian."

Charlotte didn't like the hard look Welden was giving them. He seemed to be straining to hear her explanation on why she was pulled away in the terminal.

"I'll be calling Evonne while we're still in the bay and I can get cell phone reception," Brenda said. "Maybe she'll know more than we do. She seems to know everything as soon as it happens." Evonne Clagett was the administrator of the Curtain Call retirement home, an institution Brenda and Charlotte had set up in Hopewell for retired movie actors, most of whom were indigent but still movie industry proud.

"Thought you'd gotten cold feet and stayed on shore, Charlotte," Chance called out. Marilyn nudged him hard in the ribs with her elbow and he almost spilled his drink.

"These were delivered as soon as we arrived at the cabins," Michelle said, indicating the champagne glasses. "They're called Kir Royales. A specialty of the ship, the waiter said. Came from someone named Evan Worthington, along with best wishes for your wedding. An admirer of yours, Brenda?"

"The crackers and cheese—and those bottles of champagne in the bucket over there—and the large flower basket came from the ship's cruise director, though," Brenda chirped, giving Michelle a "let's not go there" look.

"The cruise director?" Charlotte said, with a groan. "You know what that means, don't you, Brenda?"

"I told her she couldn't stay incognito on the cruise for very long," Tony said. He seemed amused.

"I'll bet they know you're on board too, Tony, so don't act so smug," Charlotte said. "Don't think you'll be escaping any glare of the spotlights that Brenda will be getting."

"Who's Evan Worthington?" Chance rang out. "The name sounds vaguely familiar."

"Shush," his wife said in a stage whisper heard across the cabin, and she nudged him in the ribs again. Whether or not Chance remembered who Worthington was, Marilyn Diamond certainly seemed to.

"That's an old friend of ours," Brenda said, giving Charlotte a sharp look not to say more.

Charlotte looked embarrassed. She knows. Brenda knows, she thought. She's probably known all along and not a hint of jealously and worry. But what she said was, "He's the chief of the Annapolis FBI office now. And, yes we are old friends back to Quantico training days."

Was that a slight gasp Charlotte had heard from Glen Welden when the FBI was mentioned. But that had only a sliver of her attention, which was focused on Evan Worthington. He was more than just an old friend, she thought. Former lovers, as well, and Evan had come to Annapolis with the stated hope that he could start up with Charlotte again—or at least that she would come back and consult with the office. She hadn't bitten on either offer. She experienced a warm feeling of gratitude, though. She recognized the drinks as a pledge of acceptance and support. When she'd told him she and Brenda were getting married and honeymooning on a Bahamas cruise, all he'd done was congratulate her, wish her happiness, and suggest that she and

Brenda would have to have one of this ship's signature drinks, a Kir Royale, as soon as they'd gotten on the ship. Ever thoughtful, he had made sure they would do so.

"Good thing you've shown up," Chance quipped. "Brenda is on her second one of these, antsy as she was that you'd run off again as soon as you let her know you'd made the sailing. We had to guard yours to keep her from drinking that too."

"I just had to check something at reception," Charlotte answered somewhat defensively. But it was true that she had left abruptly. It wasn't just remembering she was supposed to be stopping at reception; it also was seeing Brenda hooked up with an attractive man so quickly.

"I saw *you* waltzing around that one, dear," Marilyn said. "You've kept saying that Charlotte might not appear at all. You've been no help whatsoever."

"She was always late or not appearing when we grew up together," Chance retorted. But he was smiling when he said that.

"Oh shit," Tony exclaimed. He hadn't been much a part of the conversation once he saw that Charlotte had safely arrived. He had been going through the welcoming brochures and the schedule for today.

"What is it?" Brenda asked, turning to her son.

"Guess what movie is showing in the theater tonight," Tony said.

"I'm sure it's some violent shoot 'em up," Brenda said. "It's almost impossible to find a good romantic comedy or historical drama script in the making these days."

"Close enough. International intrigue, war, and murder," Tony answered.

"Sounds distasteful."

Tony laughed. "It's one of our movies, Brenda. It's the Vietnam War remake we did, *White Orchid Found*. We didn't finish the shoot, but Aaron and Howard managed to splice enough of it together to release a film this year." He referred to their longtime collaborators, Aaron Woolridge, the producer, and Howard Holton, the director.

"I hadn't heard anything about that," Brenda said.

"I think Aaron and Howard thought you didn't want to hear about that movie ever again."

"Got that right," Charlotte said, with a snort. She remembered the *White Orchid Found* movie shoot well. She'd been hired as a consultant on the movie and had wound up ferreting out a nest of spies using the filming as a cover. "You realize what this means, though, don't you?"

"It means that everyone on the ship who goes to see that movie will come back with Brenda's and my face directly in mind," Tony answered.

"Yep, that's what it means," Charlotte said. "So much for your anonymity on this cruise. And that's not all that means, either. These goodies from the cruise director . . ."

Charlotte didn't need to complete that thought. At that moment there was a rap on the door. Everyone but Chance turned their heads toward the door but took up a frozen stance. Chance opened the door to the tall figure of the ship's Norwegian captain, backed up by the sleeked-up male cruise director. The duo delivered their invitation and plea that Brenda and Tony grace the movie stage for a bow at the end of that night's showing of *White Orchid Found*.

"And Charlotte Diamond here too?" Brenda asked with a mischievous smile. Charlotte would have given her a kick if she'd been close enough to do so. "She was a consultant on the film and was instrumental in bringing it to a conclusion."

"But of course," the suave cruise director oozed with a French accent. "We'd love to include the dear lady." He was giving Charlotte a vague look, though, like he couldn't quite place where she fit in all of this, but having received an acceptance, they happily backed out of the cabin.

Charlotte puffed up to give Brenda a blast after the two men had withdrawn and closed the door, but Chance spoke up before she could.

"Can I hear another, 'oh shit'?" His feigned consternation was followed by a laugh. He obviously was very amused by it all.

"Chance, this is serious. I think you've had enough of the Kir Royales."

"It's OK and has a kick to it, but it doesn't beat a good beer as far as I'm concerned," Chance said. "And alas, I think we've drunk the last one."

"I wonder if they laid that movie on before or after ferreting out Brenda's and Tony's identities on the passenger list," Charlotte asked no one in particular. "As for getting them to invite me, Brenda—"

"You were involved in the making of the movie, too, Charlotte." Brenda said, with her signature tinkling laugh. "It never would have had an ending at all if you hadn't provided one. So you can bet I'll be dragging you up to the stage as well." And then, exhibiting her usual rosy perspective, she added, "Probably no one will go to the late movie, anyway."

"There's not that much else on the schedule this evening," Tony answered. "There are over two thousand passengers on the cruise—and not much else for them to do to wind down from the challenge of getting here in the snow."

"We'll just have to make the best of it then," Brenda said. "Maybe another one of these Kir Royales will help."

"If someone hadn't polished the last one off," Charlotte said, with a meaningful look at her brother.

The ringing of a phone somewhere in the suite startled them all at that point. Chance got up, found the phone, and answered it. "It's for you, Charlotte," he said. "Someone named Brian Harden. That name sounds familiar."

"It should, Chance. We worked together for some years. You've had dinner with him. Just as you've had dinner several times with Evan Worthington, I might add." She turned away from her brother so that he couldn't tell whether she was smiling or scowling. "Hello, Brian," she said into the phone.

"I thought this would be quicker than e-mail. The ship is still in telephone range, and I don't get charged for calls to the ship," Brian said. "I don't have anything on the murder on the last cruise yet, but I have some more background information on that wanted poster."

Charlotte listened to what Brian had to say.

"I was afraid that was the case. Yes, I've had a sighting on the cruise, I think. But perhaps, as a favor, you could just assign someone to watch until I know more of what's going on. If you'll fix it with Tim Kincaid, I'll give him the particulars. I told him what might be the case in vague terms when I met with him just now."

Brian spoke on the other end of the line for a minute.

"Yes, as a favor to me, Brian, please. Yes, I'll be careful. And, thank you."

Brenda started to speak when Charlotte replaced the receiver, but she caught Charlotte's "later" warning look. The other members of Brenda and Charlotte's entourage hadn't heard the conversation. They were busy talking over the night's schedule on the ship.

That's when Brenda reminded everyone, rather shockingly, that there was someone in the room who wasn't in the entourage. "Do have some more crackers and cheese, Glen," she said, holding a tray out to the elderly actor friend who had been sitting, eyes and ears taking it all in and smiling a little smile of contentment to himself. "There are some with delicious caviar on them. Do be sure to try those."

Charlotte looked at the man Brenda was lavishing attention on with a frown. She couldn't help but see him as an unwelcome interloper and problem. Charlotte had her problem with the attentions of Evan Worthington, certainly, but she didn't have interested suitor wannabes swirling around her like Brenda did. This was supposed to be their honeymoon, dammit.

* * * *

After seeing their guests out of the cabin door to check out their own cabins now that the Kir Royales had evaporated and the cheese and crackers had been demolished, Brenda went into the suite's bedroom to make her call to Evonne Clagett back in Hopewell. Meanwhile, Charlotte found herself being introduced to their cabin attendant, a young, very nice-looking Hispanic woman who gave her name as Eleni Hernandez. Eleni gave Charlotte a rundown on all of the services she could—and would be happy to—perform for the honeymooning couple.

Charlotte wondered if Eleni had been lurking just outside their door while she and her friends were conquering the drinks and savories just so that she could show how fast she could whisk away the ruins. If so, her intent to serve was working; Charlotte was impressed. She seemed a sweet, shy girl, ready to please—and highly capable at pleasing too, if the quickness and thoroughness of her cleaning up and exiting the cabin was any indication. She wasn't the wonder woman that their own housekeeper, Bea Helgerson was, of course—but no one was.

As Eleni was leaving the suite, Brenda came in from the bedroom, her cell phone in her hand and a quizzical look on her face.

"Everything OK at Curtain Call?" Charlotte asked.

"No, not really," Brenda answered in a hesitant voice. "Evonne hasn't heard anything we didn't already know about the Russian diplomat killed at the Vales' B&B, but she had other disturbing news, closer to home."

"Oh?"

"It's Zenna. She hasn't shown up at work at Curtain Call, and Evonne couldn't find her either at her home or her café on Main Street."

"Has she reported—?"

"Evonne said she called the sheriff, but he said Zenna hadn't been missing long enough for him to be involved—and she said he seemed to be preoccupied with the Russian case."

"And she didn't say he'd made any connection between Zenna's disappearance and the Russian being shot and the two other Russians probably stealing our limousine and skipping town in the snow?"

"No, she didn't. Should he have?"

"Zenna's Russian," Charlotte said, trying to control her exasperation. "And I think I've told you that Zenna was brought to the States and hidden away in Hopewell by the CIA—by the CIA official Win Engleton, who lived on the point, where Curtain Call now is. So, yes, if a Russian diplomat shows up dead in Hopewell, chances are good that it's connected with Zenna. Why else would a Russian diplomat be in Hopewell? It can't very well be for Win. The Russians think he's dead. If the CIA brought

54

Zenna here, it most likely was because she had been working for them in Russia, and the Russians hardly could be happy about that."

"So, you think the Russians were there because of Zenna and she might be in trouble?"

"I think she very well might be worse than in trouble if they got to her before the Russian was killed. And, if not, she may be missing because the Russian was killed."

"You mean she might have—?"

"There's always that possibility. Anything is possible until it has been discounted."

Charlotte looked through the sliding glass doors out onto the balcony. It was getting dark, but she could see the shoreline to the east of the ship. They were still in the Chesapeake Bay. Her cell phone should still work.

"I've got to make a call. I'd have to dig for my cell phone. Can I use yours?"

"Certainly. Here," Brenda said, handing her phone to Charlotte. There was no use even suggesting that Charlotte look for her own. She hadn't been in her luggage yet and she ascribed to the packing school of opening the lid and throwing everything at the suitcase until the lid couldn't be closed any more. And then Charlotte always wondered why she looked so wrinkled when they traveled. Brenda would say something, but she didn't want to be a nag and, for truth, she liked Charlotte just the way she was. "Are you calling Haws?"

"The sheriff is hopeless—especially if he hasn't connected the dots himself." Charlotte dialed the phone. "Please be there, David," she said while the phone was ringing.

David Burch, one of the deputy sheriffs of the county Hopewell was in, Talbot County, and the deputy mostly responsible for the Hopewell area, picked up the line. "David. We've heard from Evonne that Zenna is missing. Chances are good she's why the Russians were in Hopewell."

"I thought that too," the deputy answered. "I've tried to make the connection with the sheriff, but he's not having it yet. He thinks she's just off somewhere with Grady and that they'll both turn up."

"With Grady? Grady Tarbell? Why would she—?"

"You didn't know? They're an item. I've tried to find her everywhere I know of, including at Grady's house, and—"

"They're a couple? I didn't know that. I seem to be the last to know anything happening in Hopewell like that. That pins it down even more then. You need to track them down—both of them."

"Why? What do you mean that pins the case down?"

"Grady was at the B&B when the Russian was killed. His car went off the road by the house and he was taken into the Vales' for supper. If the Russians were there to do harm to Zenna, and he suspected that—and if he's involved with Zenna—"

"I get it. This should convince the sheriff. Thanks, Ms. Diamond. You continue to be the sharpest mind in Talbot County even when you're not there."

"I hope I'm wrong, David. But I hope Zenna's safe as well."

She clicked off and handed the cell phone back to Brenda, who was looking slightly stricken.

"I'm afraid—"

"No need to tell me," Brenda said. "I could clearly hear the conversation. What are we going to do?"

"It's our honeymoon, Brenda. We're going to dress and go to dinner and let this work itself out. There's nothing we can do for either Zenna or Grady at the moment. David will let me know as soon as they make some progress. We're on our honeymoon. We're going to dress and meet the rest for dinner and not say—or think, if that's possible—any more about this this evening."

As circumstances would have it, Charlotte was almost immediately propelled into other mysteries closer to hand than dead Russians, missing CIA assets, and a supposedly stodgy professor.

* * * *

"So far so good," Marilyn whispered as they walked into the depths of the ship's dining room. They arrived a little later than the assigned hour because it had taken them a while to form up in Charlotte and Brenda's suite. They all had the same table assignment, but the tables were of various sizes so they had no idea whether it would only be the six of them at table.

They would have been there sooner but when they got to an entrance into a stairwell, they encountered Eleni Hernandez, assigned to all of their cabins as room attendant, and she greeted each of them by name. She was almost finished with her litany of names when her expression suddenly changed to a look that almost seemed to Charlotte to be fear and Eleni stumbled past them in the narrow corridor and disappeared into a cabin with an open door, which she evidently had been servicing.

The six gave questioning looks to each other and it was only when Charlotte rounded the corridor corner to where she could see into the stairwell that she saw a couple of the suspicious-looking young Hispanic men she'd observed communicating with each other in the terminal moving up the stairs toward the Galleon Café on the deck nine pool deck. She almost shrank from them as they gave her party the evil eye. And this reaction made her wonder if that's what had sent Eleni scurrying into a cabin as well.

Their table proved to be in the center of the deck four main floor of the dining room and was an oval table seating ten. The four others assigned to the table were already in place when they approached. They had actually arrived at a good time. Most of the other diners were being served their appetizers and wine and only a few heads lifted as they passed. A large number of these diners, though, gave the party a quizzical look as if halfway recognizing one or the other of them, but not quite sure why they did.

They had barely made it to the table and been introduced to their other four tablemates—the ship's cruise director, Eduard Pierce, who had come to Brenda and Charlotte's suite earlier; the director of the ship's stage troupe, Sheila Sheridan; and Joseph and Ann Crawford, Joseph being a manufacturer of something or other that obviously was very profitable—when an enthusiastic squeal from a nearby table arrested the attention of all.

"It's her, Daddy. I know it's her." The voice was that of a young girl.

"Uh, oh, the gig is up," Marilyn muttered.

Charlotte moved toward Brenda as if to shield her, if necessary.

As their eyes focused, a young girl of seven or eight bounced toward the table, making a beeline in Brenda's direction—but bypassing her and winding up in front of Michelle Minor.

Brenda's laughter combined with Michelle's as the girl declared, "It's you, isn't it? The tennis star. I followed all of your matches at Wimbledon last year. You were so bundled up before we got on the boat and you were saying nice things to me that I didn't know it was you. I thought you looked familiar but I didn't know it was you. But it *is* you, isn't it?"

"Yes, you caught me, I am me," Michelle said with a smile as the young girl reached her. She and the others in the party recognized the girl as the one they met briefly while in the passport control line in the terminal. "And what would your name be? And do you play tennis?"

"I'm Bonnie," the young girl declared. "And I was taking tennis lessons. I was taking them before . . ." She didn't complete that sentence, though, suddenly looking a bit stricken and looking around as a young man approached her.

"I'm so sorry," the man said, swiveling his head around to make his apologies clear to all in Brenda and Charlotte's party. "Bonnie, sweetheart, it's not polite to be so forward. Let's let this folks enjoy their dinner. Maybe you'll see Miss . . ."

"It's Michelle Minor, the tennis star, Daddy," Bonnie said breathlessly.

"Well, perhaps you can see her at the pool someday."

"Can I?" the little girl said, turning her hopeful face to Michelle.

"I'd like that. I'll be looking for you at the pool," Michelle said, flashing the young girl a big smile.

"Thank the nice people and come back to our table now," the man said as he coaxed Bonnie away.

Brenda could barely hold her laughter as the man and his daughter turned back to their table.

"Guess you dodged a bullet so far," Chance said to the movie star.

"Maybe that's the way the whole cruise will be," Brenda said. "Maybe it will be Michelle and Tony that they all know. There are so many young people on board because of the school holiday that I might as well be from another world to them." And, indeed, although Michelle hadn't been receiving knowing looks, Tony certainly had been. But then, Tony was such a heartthrob that he'd always get looks from women anyway—and some men as well.

"Only until about midnight tonight, I'm sure," Tony said. "After you take the stage for a bow after the movie showing tonight, I'm sure you'll be the center of attention for the rest the cruise. Don't you think so, Charlotte?"

But Charlotte's mind was preoccupied and had been ever since the young girl and the man had approached the table. This was the girl and man who had caught her attention in the departure terminal and then caused a jolt of recognition when she'd been looking at the wanted posters in Brian Harden's office.

Well, perhaps it was good that they had established a connection, she thought. She needed to talk to this man privately and then decide what she must do.

Chapter Five: Exposure at the Pool

Brenda, Charlotte and their entourage had quite a night at the movies. *White Orchid Found* hadn't turned out half bad as a movie, even Charlotte had to admit. There had been some marvelous editing, cutting, and rearranging done there. There had to be a lot of editing; the filming as scheduled had never been completed. After the viewing the packed theater had gone wild when Brenda had been announced by the cruise director and brought to the stage—followed by Tony and Charlotte, as having worked with the film too. Michelle came with her own celebrity value, of course, and the audience was made to feel like it was getting insider "news" first, as the tabloids hadn't caught on to Tony and Michelle dating yet. Brenda had even brought up Glen Welden, who received a better second-wind reception from the audience after Brenda had mentioned the unforgettable films he'd been in, albeit in mostly forgettable support roles.

They had gotten to bed at an ungodly hour, and, to Charlotte's disappointment, Brenda had gone to sleep as soon as her head hit the pillow. Charlotte's head was full of multiple mysteries, though, so she hadn't slept so quickly or soundly. None of this was original or unique to being on the sea. Brenda always slept late when she could manage it, and Charlotte had always been a light sleeper.

Early the next afternoon, Charlotte was dragged nearly kicking and screaming out to the open-air pool area on the ninth and tenth decks, where the activities director had made sure that six prominently displayed lounge beds were available to them in an otherwise teeming area beside the main pool where territorial wars were constantly under way over position. She hadn't wanted to come and Brenda had to almost literally pull her away from the computer where she was burning up what would be very expensive Internet time if she hadn't been given a free account by the ship's security chief.

As she grunted and groaned her way into a bathing suit that wouldn't have been out of place on the Atlantic Beach boardwalk in the 1920s, Charlotte groused about her Internet discussions and her phone call to the FBI office in Annapolis.

It had been anything but a discussion with David Burch over the Russian diplomat murder case and the disappearance of Zenna Brodsky and Grady Tarbell. David had uncharacteristically gone silent until in her third message Charlotte managed to get him to admit that Sheriff Haws Wainwright had put a gag order on him and all of the other deputies on the status of the investigation.

"But did he buy the connection of the Russian shooting and Zenna and Grady's disappearances?" Charlotte asked. And all she'd gotten in return was, "I'm sorry Ms. Diamond, he won't even say anything about any of this to me. He just says that it's out of our hands."

Aha, Charlotte thought. She knew exactly what that meant, and she knew that it wasn't David Burch who was stonewalling her. And she also knew where to go next.

But after Charlotte had gotten through the niceties of thanking him for the Kir Royales he'd had sent to their suite to send them off from Baltimore, her good friend and former lover, Evan Worthington, the agent in charge of the FBI's Annapolis office, wasn't any more help on the particulars when she e-mailed him.

"How is the cruise? I was told there was to be no business while you were on your honeymoon," was his first response. "And I do believe, Charlotte, that you were the one who told me that. I wouldn't dare go against anything Charlotte Diamond pledged me to do."

"Very funny, Evan. And every evasive," Charlotte responded. "So, it's true. The FBI has stepped in to that case. Because of the Russian diplomat? Or because of Zenna Brodsky—and the Russians? At least tell me that you can see that the shooting is related to the disappearances."

"I could only discuss that with an official consultant with the FBI, Ms. Diamond," Worthington answered. "Are you ready to come back on board?"

Charlotte hadn't bothered to answer that. She already basically had her answer. The feds had taken the case up. And if they hadn't already linked Zenna's disappearance to the death of the Russian diplomat—likely only if Haws Wainwright hadn't apprised the bureau of Zenna's disappearance—they certainly would be doing so now. That's all that Charlotte could ask for from this distance.

Even without an answer, Worthington had followed up with a, "Well then. Let me know when you want to go official again."

It had been at that point that Brenda, coming in from the balcony, where she had been polishing off the breakfast she'd ordered delivered to the room, the Galleon Café now being closed to prepare for lunch, had tracked Charlotte down and declared that they were to meet Tony and Michelle—and maybe Chance and Marilyn, as well—at the pool.

When they got there, moving through a scattered crowd of young and not so young women ogling Tony as he stretched out on his lounge bed, in a Speedo, and showing as much as a movie star romantic lead could be expected to exhibit, Charlotte saw that only Tony and Michelle had arrived. Removing the reserved signs the cruise director had put on the beds, she and Brenda took the lounge beds at the opposite end of the string from Tony and Michelle, with Charlotte trying her best not to look like any part of the glamorous party at all.

She didn't try too hard to separate herself, though, for Brenda's sake. Charlotte was still touched from the previous evening when Brenda hadn't let her fade into the shadows during the movie curtain call. She'd been deeply embarrassed to be brought forward with Brenda's arm laced in hers, but she could only think upon Brenda with the deepest love as Brenda had bravely and fiercely informed everyone in the theater that this was their honeymoon cruise—that she and Charlotte were married. Charlotte knew that Brenda must have lost some fans by declaring that, but Brenda had said that the whole point of them getting married when Maryland laws permitted was because they didn't want to hide their union from the world, and that anyone who wasn't happy with that could just go hang. She said she wouldn't flaunt it, but she wouldn't hide it, either, and that Charlotte had been key to filming of *White Orchid Found*. Charlotte hadn't been sure that Brenda meant that until that very moment, on the stage, in front of possibly more than a thousand passengers who they'd be stuck with, for good or ill, for several days.

The applause that had responded to Brenda's announcement gave Charlotte some hope that the world, indeed, was changing.

So, as much as it pained her and as much as she didn't consider herself in anywhere near the league of the movie star, Charlotte was not shrinking from appearing with Brenda at the pool. Nothing else besides this feeling of obligation to stand firm with Brenda would have gotten Charlotte into the bathing suit she had taken with her all over the globe for the last ten years—but had never been brave enough to wear in public.

No sooner than they had become positioned, however, with two open, but reserved lounge beds between the honeymooning couple and Tony and Michelle, awaiting the possible arrival of Charlotte's brother and his wife, than Charlotte was struck with doubts again. The elderly actor, Glen Welden, had appeared and settled, seated, on the lounge beside Brenda, and the two had immediately struck up a deep conversation about mutual actor friends and the state of Hollywood in general. As good as Welden looked in a natty suit, he looked even better in a bathing suit. He was fit and tanned and had a broad white-toothed smile that got the attention of any woman passing by who was over fifty.

He obviously was a few years older than Brenda and Charlotte, but he seemed to have blossomed overnight. Whereas he had seemed withdrawn and shy when Charlotte had first encountered him on a stairwell landing upon arrival on the ship—almost, Charlotte would have said, stealthy looking—his encounters with Brenda and Brenda's inclusion of him at the post-movie bows the previous evening had obviously pumped confidence into him.

Maybe too much confidence, Charlotte thought, as she watched his animated conversation with Brenda. It almost was like Charlotte wasn't here at the moment, and that Brenda had slipped into her old life as a premier movie actress. This had always been a danger to both women—that they had met at the end of their disparate careers rather than when they could share their professional worlds. There were similarities between a life in the movies and that of a senior FBI agent, but it was hard when you had accumulated thirty years of adventures in those lives before meeting not to drift off into your own world. Brenda had shown that she instinctively knew that Charlotte was drawn to crime cases and also, for that matter, to Evan Worthington, although Charlotte didn't think that Brenda understood how deeply she and Evan had once been involved. And for Charlotte's part, just as she was observing now, it seemed that Brenda could so easily be reabsorbed into the movie world that Charlotte had to continually fear at such times that Brenda would realize she missed that world so much that she had to go back. Charlotte didn't want to live in Hollywood—although, of course, if that's where Brenda was going to live, so would she. If Brenda wanted Charlotte in Hollywood. Charlotte knew that she was too prone to give a lot of credence to the world "if."

It wasn't an empty fear. Brenda had gone back to the movies, if only briefly, more than once since she and Charlotte had met. And each time Charlotte had harbored the fear that Brenda wouldn't return to the relatively quiet life, other than a mystery or murder to two, of Hopewell-on-the-Choptank. At the same time, Charlotte had to acknowledge that her own continued falling into a case of crime—just as she now had, and concerning more than one case—must be seen by Brenda as a danger. Charlotte had been drawn strongly to Evan Worthington's request that she become an official consultant to the FBI Annapolis office, but the main reason she hadn't taken up the offer was for fear that Brenda would see that as a defeat for their attempt to form a whole new life with each other.

It wasn't helping today that Glen Welden looked so damn good for his age and that he and Brenda were having a grand time gossiping about the movie world. Jealous and frustrated as she was, though, as she stretched out on the lounge bed, covering her legs with towels as much so they couldn't be seen as that they didn't burn, Charlotte felt herself sinking into cogitations about the various police cases she had let herself become embroiled in. She dozed off under the rays of the sun and the background noise of the pool activity thinking about the visit she would be making to what she had termed the "murder cabin" later in the afternoon. She thought it probably was a waste of time for her to look for any clues in that cabin that the authorities might have overlooked. But one never knew.

Don Welden had just risen from the lounge bed next to Brenda's and was talking of needing to go back to his cabin for what he called "the obligatory afternoon nap of the elderly," which caught Charlotte's attention and brought her out of her reverie about the murder on the previous cruise. She was one to covet an afternoon nap herself, but she really didn't like to be reminded about its connection to the elderly. She had never worried about growing old before she met Brenda. Now, however, she tried to capture every minute of the time she had left on earth, every minute she could spend with Brenda.

As Welden was leaving, the Blaines, father and daughter, were passing by on the walking track that ran along the rail on the deck overlooking the pool area, and seeing them on the track above, Brenda hailed them and urged them to come down for a visit.

Bonnie Blaine needed no repeated invitation and began pulling on her somewhat reluctant father's arm directing him to a set of stairs and down to the pool area where Brenda and Charlotte's party had prominent places.

"Are you finding enough activities to amuse you?" Brenda asked Bonnie when she reached them. The young girl went almost immediately to Michelle's lounge bed, and the young tennis star put away the novel she'd been reading and sat up on the side of her lounge. She patted the cushion next to her and Bonnie plopped down. She was bouncing up and down in excitement, though. "We had a special tour of the ship this morning, and I've been to a class where we made a necklace out of sea shells. See, I made this one. And I was in a water polo game just before lunch, and Daddy found a café near the back of the boat that makes ice cream sundaes, and later this afternoon he said there's a trivia game in the Seamaster Lounge. And then after that . . . after that . . . Daddy, I don't remember what comes after that."

Bonnie, her eyes wide with energy and pleasure, looked up at her father, who was still standing at the foot of the lounge beds, looking apologetic for them having interjected themselves in the group despite Brenda's invitation that they do so. Charlotte's heart went out to the Blaines. There obviously was a very close bond between father and daughter, and Charlotte felt deep regret at the conundrum she faced with them.

"Oh, my, you're having a busy cruise," Brenda said, bestowing one of her signature laughs on those about her. The laugh was loud and distinctive enough that a few on surrounding lounge beds looked up, startled, at hearing a laugh that they only heard in the movies.

It was that moment that the cruise director, standing in front of a microphone, by the diving boards at the deep end of the pool, blew into the mike and called for everyone's attention, saying what a special treat it was to have on this cruise the movie stars Brenda Brandon and Tony Trice. He said that if the applause was loud enough maybe the two would be willing to come forward to the mike and talk a bit with him and maybe even take some questions from those at the pool.

Brenda blushed at being called out, but, of course, she was gracious enough to sit up on the lounge bed, gesture to Tony, and, with him, to walk to the mike. Charlotte wasn't fooled by the blush. She knew that, ever the trouper, Brenda had an area in the back of her brain that appreciated and sought the recognition. For Tony's part, he didn't have to be asked twice. He had bounded up and put out a hand to help Brenda rise. Charlotte could see that most of the eyes of the women were on Tony as they went forward to the mike. He had a towel draped around his neck, but it didn't do much to hide the physique that made many a viewer swoon for his heartthrob roles in the movies. In any event, all attention on the pool deck was riveted to the two movie stars as they moved forward.

Charlotte took a deep breath. This was an opportunity, and the longer she put off what she had to do, the harder it would be to do it and the longer it would fester and mar her honeymoon cruise.

"Bonnie," she called over to Michelle's lounge bed when the applause had died and the cruise director started asking Brenda questions at the mike, "I think Michelle said she'd show you her tennis racket and maybe give you a few pointers. If you can fit her into your busy schedule, perhaps right now would be a good time for you two to do that."

Michelle looked a bit startled by the suggestion and gave Charlotte a quizzical look. She got an imploring look in turn. She was quick on the uptake, though, and said. "Oh, yes, let's . . . if you're interested . . . and your father can spare you for a few minutes."

Bonnie's eyes when right to her father, "Can I, Daddy? Please, Please?"

Don Blaine laughed, gave a sigh of resignation, and said. "Sure, sweetheart. Whatever you want . . . as long as it isn't an imposition on Ms. Minor."

"Certainly it isn't," Michelle answered, with a smile. "We'll have a grand time. Where and when can we meet you?"

"You can come right back here when you're done," Charlotte quickly said. "Mr. Blaine can stay here and keep me company. It looks like Brenda and Tony are in for the duration."

As Michelle and Bonnie walked away—Michelle almost gliding in a manner that was both like a dancer and like an athlete and Bonnie skipping excitedly at her side—Charlotte and Don Blaine, the only two remaining at the lounge beds at this point, tuned back into the question and answer session at the mike beside the pool in time to hear the cruise director deftly maneuver Brenda into agreeing to sing a couple of songs during the early show of the Caribbean Singers and Dancers troupe at the

Neptune Theater the evening after next, after the ship had departed Cape Canaveral for the Bahamas.

"Oh lordy," Charlotte declared. "So much for a quiet pleasure cruise." But she quickly turned back to Don Blaine. "Please, Mr. Blaine, have a seat on one of the lounge beds. Please. It will be much too long a wait for Bonnie to return for you to be standing there."

Blaine was looking off in the direction of his disappearing daughter, and once more Charlotte's heart went out to him. He almost looked bereft, as if he couldn't bear having his daughter out of his sight for even a moment.

"She's a lovely child," Charlotte said in a low voice when Blaine was seated.

"Yes, yes, she is. She's a treasure," he answered.

"You and her mother must be very proud of her."

There was a pause, and then Blaine answered, "Yes, we are." He wasn't looking at Charlotte, though. Once again he was looking toward where he'd last seen Bonnie walking away with Michelle.

"But Bonnie doesn't know that her mother isn't aware that she's on this cruise with you, does she?"

"I beg your pardon?" Blaine said, snapping his attention around to Charlotte. Looking more guilty than confused.

"I have connections with law enforcement. I've seen your face on wanted posters. For child kidnapping."

There was a long pause and Blaine made as if to rise and walk away. But, with a sigh, he settled back down. They were on a ship on the open seas. There was no place to escape to. "It's nothing like kidnapping," he answered at length. "It's more complicated than that."

"Believe me," Charlotte answered, "if I couldn't see how Bonnie worships you and how you react with her, you'd already be in police custody. As it is, ship security is keeping an eye on you. I don't think you would want to try anything desperate—anything that would endanger or upset Bonne. I can see you aren't doing the child any harm; I've had enough experience with that to tell when a child has worries or is trying to hide some form of abuse.

Is this the only way you could see her, though? Snatch her from her mother?"

"Yes, basically. I wouldn't want Bonnie to know for the world—she thinks that Ginny has given permission for us to go on this cruise. It's something Bonnie has really wanted to do, and her mother has been too preoccupied to hear her. I promised to take Bonnie on a cruise before all of this happened with Ginny. And at the office. And with the police in Tampa."

There was a long pause before Blaine spoke again. "I knew it would be just this one time—and that it would end up badly for me. But, if not, I would have had no time at all with Bonnie. And I promised her this cruise." He turned to Charlotte. "What now? The cruise has just started. It stops at Cape Canaveral tomorrow. I guess . . ."

"I think the end of the cruise, back in Baltimore, should be soon enough," Charlotte answered in a low voice. "I don't see what the harm would be in waiting until then, as long as you don't make it difficult. Ship security will watch, but not obtrusively. I can see that Bonnie needs and deserves this time with you. She'll have it very rough after this, poor child."

"Yes, I know," Blaine said in a voice choked with emotion. "And . . . thank you." He had his hands up to his face and was looking down at the deck rather than at Charlotte. He was about to add something, when they were joined by Chance and Marilyn, who had come at last to claim their places by the pool.

The suspense in time was long enough that Charlotte knew that, if the man was going to include a justification that made his wife out the center of the blame for the situation, he would have done so. And she marked it in his favor that he didn't make her a scapegoat in this way.

In the boisterous swirl of their appearance, with Marilyn showing Charlotte the "steals" she had found in the shopping arcade and Chance rolling his eyes at knowing better but not speaking up because he didn't want to spoil his wife's pleasure, Don Blaine managed to pull himself together and to smile wanly and respond appropriately to questions on his opinion of how well the top and slacks that Marilyn had pulled out of a sales bin coordinated.

Charlotte looked around the pool area, noticing how intently everyone was still drinking in the impromptu performance of Brenda and Tony at the mike. This almost uniform focus on the two movie stars helped the others pop out to Charlotte as anomalies. The young Hispanic men, in bathing suits that normally would allow them to blend in, were scattered around the periphery of the pool area. None of them were looking at Brenda and Tony; all seemed to be scoping out the others at the pool— with frequent looks at each other. They had devices that looked like cell phones, but the ship was out of cell phone range now, so they must be some sort of mobile phones that were networked with each other.

Only one of them wasn't involved in this surveillance. Charlotte saw him in an open hatchway into one of the ship's stair halls—and she had seen him because of the violent way he was shaking a woman by the arm and talking intently at her. It took Charlotte a moment to realize that the woman was Eleni Hernandez, their room attendant. Charlotte started to rise from the lounge bed, but just as she did, the Q&A session with Brenda and Tony was breaking up, and the crowd's attention was being freed and scattered. The Hispanic youths were blending into the now-chattering teeming mass swirling around the pool. Eleni had disappeared into the ship's interior, and her assailant had melted into the crowd.

So intent had Charlotte been on the young Hispanics that she had missed seeing Glen Welden. He hadn't gone straight to his cabin after he'd left Brenda's side. He'd sought out the cruise director and suggested that Brenda would be amenable to the Q&A activity that just had happened, and then, as the crowd became mesmerized by Brenda and Tony, he's taken a winding route back to his cabin. A route that went from one beach bag or purse to another, and all positioned well enough from the protective view of their owners for him to collect some purloined goodies to take back with him into the bowels of the ship to assess and gloat over.

Chapter Six: The Murder Cabin

Later that afternoon, with Brenda taking a nap after they'd returned from the pool, Charlotte slipped away to the deck below. She used the sea pass card Kincaid had given her to enter the murder scene cabin, which she slowly walked through, clicking into a detective's observation mode. Her attention was first arrested by the chalk mark on the carpet outlining the position of the woman's body. There were blood stains in and around it. There were blood stains too in the chair just a few feet from where the body had dropped. The chair was where the husband had been found, stabbed several times and nearly gone when the attendant had opened the door, thinking that the couple had departed their cabin to wait in their designated departure lounge while the passengers were systematically being disembarked from the ship in Baltimore harbor.

There was something not quite right about the positioning of the body, Charlotte thought. Something about the detailed report of what had been found in the cabin, something not there now. She looked around, trying to go through the report in her mind and compare what was then and what was now. It didn't take her long to uncover what it was. When the attendant had entered the cabin the door to the balcony had been open. It was closed now, of course. They couldn't just leave it open with the ship under way. The wind-driven salt air would have ruined the interior of the cabin.

That clicked with Charlotte. Could she perhaps tell whether the murder had occurred when the ship was under way or after it had returned to dock at Baltimore? The attendant hadn't serviced the room for more than a day because the "do not disturb" sign had been out, so the time of the attack hadn't been pinned down yet. With an "umpf" and appreciation she was in the cabin alone, Charlotte worked her way down on her knees by the sofa about five feet inside the door to the balcony. Again glad no one else was there she felt the carpet and lowered her face to take sniff. Yes, it was damp, which it would be anyway, but it smelled salty. And she traced the dampness all the way over to the bed. Because damp and salty air had made it that far while the door was open, chances were good the ship had been under way at the time.

She started to try to get up, but she didn't quite make it the first time. As she fell back on her haunches, the chalk outline between her and the chair where the husband had been found caught her attention. The woman's head had been toward the room. The knife had been found between the body and where the husband was sitting in the chair. The assumption of the forensics team was that the husband had dropped it as he sank into his chair after having fought with his wife, mortally wounding her and being stabbed himself in her fruitless struggle for survival.

But, Charlotte thought, why was the balcony door open and why, if the two had been struggling inside that open door, had the wife fallen facing into the room? If they'd pulled apart and the husband, stabbed himself, had sunk into the chair, why wasn't the wife moving away from him, toward possible safety, and why hadn't she fallen either between him and the cabin door or facing away from him toward the balcony door?

Charlotte struggled to her feet and moved out onto the balcony, careful to look where she was walking and where her hands went. She found what she half anticipated she would find. There were blood stains on the balcony railing. So, the fight hadn't only been in the room. But this made the orientation of the bodies even more curious. She also noticed that, at the base of the railing, some of the blood was streaked toward the door, further evidence that the ship was under way with wind blowing in toward the cabin.

She left the cabin and went to the reception desk and asked that the ship's security chief, Tim Kincaid, be summoned. She was led immediately to his office in a small warren of cubicles between the back of the reception desk area and the casino.

"So, you've examined the cabin," Kincaid said when Charlotte was seated across from him. "Were you able to come to any conclusions?"

"I didn't see references to blood stains on the balcony railing in the forensics report," she said. "Do you know if the team realized they were there?"

"That's odd," Kincaid said. "Do you have your copy of the report with you?"

Charlotte produced it.

"Ah, you're missing a few pages. Yes, those blood stains are listed in the full report."

"Do you know if they have been typed and compared with the couple's blood?"

"Yes, that's being done. We haven't received the results yet, though. We have, however ascertained the name of the man the wife was seen drinking with more than once. He was French. Philippe LeJoie, was the name on his passport."

"What was found in his cabin? I take it his luggage wasn't there."

"It was the last night of the voyage. Everyone's luggage had been set out to start being offloaded as soon as the ship docked in Baltimore the next day. There was a carry-on bag in his room, though, and toiletries and a change of clothes and a clothes bag. We figure he abandoned them and somehow got off the ship as soon as it docked—that he might have been involved in the fight and could, in fact, have assaulted both the husband and the wife. The husband wasn't conscious yet the last I knew. We should know much more when the Baltimore police are able to interview him, assuming he survives. But it remains a mystery how LeJoie could have gotten off the ship. His sea pass card record wasn't in the departure system. He may have passed himself off as a luggage handler and left that way."

"I think you should get in contact with Brian Harden in Baltimore and ask him to get the blood on the railing typed as soon as possible." Charlotte said. "I think chances are good that Philip LeJoie left the ship another way."

"Oh?"

"I think it's possible that LeJoie was in on the plot to murder the husband, but got cold feet and interrupted the wife trying to kill the husband—it will be a more assured theory if it's her fingerprints that are prominent on the knife handle—and that the mortal stabbing of the wife occurred during a struggle with the boyfriend on the balcony. It could be that the wife was coming back into the cabin from the balcony when she collapsed and died."

"That would mean, then—"

"Yes, that, just maybe, the boyfriend went over the railing and into the water as the ship was sailing up the Chesapeake Bay toward Baltimore that night. It's possible that he was in on the plot and got cold feet or maybe even that the wife was setting him up to take the fall for murdering her husband. This may not be a plot to murder the wife, but, rather, a failed plot to murder the husband."

Chapter Seven: Fire on the Water!

"Hurry and finish getting dressed, Charlotte," Brenda called from the suite's living room. "We're at the captain's table tonight, and I'm quite sure we are all supposed to be in place before the captain arrives."

"Is that Eleni you're talking to out there," Charlotte asked, her voice sounding huffy. "Damn, I knew I should have ordered this dress two sizes larger or brought a girdle."

"Does anyone wear girdles anymore?" Brenda called back with a laugh.

"Says the woman who never needed one. Is Eleni out there?"

"She was, but she's gone."

"Damn. The woman's a phantom. I've been wanting to talk to her."

"About what? She's well trained. Everything gets done and she's never in evidence."

"If you ask me, she's avoiding us. And I just want to talk to her, that's all." Charlotte didn't see a need to worry Brenda with her concern about the gang—she thought of them as a gang—of young Hispanic men and about one of them having contact with their room attendant. The men were totally out of place on this cruise. This was a pleasure cruise, and each time Charlotte had seen them, they had been tense and seemed to be casing the passengers. She was concerned about that.

And now she had even more reason to be concerned about it. When she had checked in with the ship's security chief, Tim Kincaid, as the ship had been pulling out of Cape Canaveral, headed for the Bahamas, two hours earlier, Kincaid not only told her that her theory about the death of the woman on the previous cruise, as the ship had been returning to Baltimore, had been spot on, but also that he was worried about a rash of thefts on the ship since they had sailed. Kincaid had confirmed that the boyfriend, LeJoie, hadn't turned up yet, that the blood on the balcony railing and the floor of the balcony matched his DNA, and that prints from all three were on the knife but that the wife's were the most prominent.

"Sorry about the thefts," Charlotte had said. "But I can't help you much there. That's below the threshold of anything I've worked on."

"Some pretty valuable items have been taken, Ms. Diamond, but I understand that you must be on overload now on more serious cases."

You have no idea, Charlotte had thought. But what she said was, "Ah, grand larceny rather than petty larceny then. I'll keep my eyes open." She had to acknowledge that it wasn't the first grand larceny theft circumstance she'd faced while traveling on water. She'd encountered quirky diamond thieves on a Christmas cruise down the Rhine in Germany a few years earlier.

Another vacation nearly ruined by my inability to keep my nose out of crime going on under my nose, she had thought as she moved swiftly back to her suite, knowing she had to start trying to pour herself into a formal dress. She was not pleased when they'd received an invitation to sit at the captain's table at the first of two gala captain's dinners during the cruise. She had been hoping to skip the formal dinner and snack at the Galleon Café instead—along with nearly half of the others on the cruise who came for the sun and beach, not to show off tuxedos and formals.

Not being able to track down Eleni to ask her about the Hispanic gang had only added to her irritation, especially when the choices panned out to be to go into the suite's living room when she heard Brenda talking to Eleni—and trying to think of some way gracefully to get rid of Brenda so she could talk to Eleni alone—and getting this long dress she'd bought to cover her belly and her rear quarters at the same time, on without overstressing the material.

And then, when she had just built up a satisfying "mad," she walked into the living room and Brenda had whistled and said, "You look terrific, Charlotte." That, of course, had deflated her irritation completely. It didn't matter that she didn't think it was true, she had become convinced that Brenda did think it was true—that no matter what Charlotte wore, Brenda would always think she was beautiful. That was what love was all about—and that was why they were on this honeymoon cruise.

They were surprised to find when they got to the dining room that the captain's table was the same center-dining room table they sat at for their regular dinners. Their companions—Chance and Marilyn and Tony and Michelle—were also there, as were the billionaire manufacturer of "whatever," Joseph Crawford, and his wife, Ann. The only change was that instead of the cruise director and the stage company director, the captain, Sven Arnholdt, and his first officer were there.

The captain was quite personable—and quite taken with Brenda, although Charlotte didn't feel as threatened by his attentions to her "other" as she had when Glen Welden was buzzing around Brenda. The captain, a Norwegian who spent his entire life on the sea, was from an entirely different world. Brenda's blind spot in attraction was with people in the movies. Up until she'd met Charlotte, she'd proven that time and time again.

Charlotte was curious, though, that the captain and Tony kept exchanging knowing glances and even that once the captain referred to a surprise they shared—but weren't going to share it with the others right now. Charlotte was almost afraid that Tony had requested that the ship do something special to publicly acknowledge that she and Brenda were on their honeymoon—which both of the women had adamantly requested not be done—but other than that niggling little concern, Charlotte was enjoying herself too much to launch into her usual analysis. It was obvious that neither Tony nor the captain were going to reveal anything further about their surprise.

Charlotte pressed Brenda for some alone time—just the two of them—at the Brigantine bar after dinner and before the floor show in the Neptune Theater, where Brenda had agreed to sing three songs.

"You looked like you were having a good time at dinner, Charlotte," Brenda said when they were settled, each with a Kir Royale, and listening to quiet piano playing in the background. They were sitting by a floor-to-ceiling window looking out onto the moon reflecting across the gently rolling waves of the Atlantic

Ocean right up to where they were sitting in the ship. "It's good to see you without worries, and smiling."

"I wasn't smiling," Charlotte said. "I was grimacing. This dress is hellishly tight around the middle."

"You can't fool me. You were enjoying yourself."

"Yes, I was, but I'm afraid I didn't pull you in here for a private chat for either of us to enjoy ourselves."

"Oh, what's wrong, Charlotte?"

And then Charlotte told Brenda about the Blaines—that Don Blaine, who was in a very acrimonious visitation rights battle with his estranged wife had snatched his daughter from the wife's Tampa home and was the subject of a massive hunt. The wife was claiming that the father was a danger to Bonnie, that he was unbalanced and had threatened to kill the daughter if the wife didn't take him back.

"Oh, I don't believe that for a moment," Brenda said. "You've seen how devoted those two are to each other, and Don Blaine shows absolutely no signs of being unbalanced. Believe me, an actress can tell when a man is covering up a bad nature. If he's threatened to kill anyone, it's probably the wife, for being a grasping witch."

"I quite agree," Charlotte answered. "If I didn't, I would have had him arrested before the ship left Baltimore. I recognized his face on a poster in Brian Harden's office in the terminal building. Brian would have pulled him off the ship right then if I hadn't asked him to hold off. And I'm glad I did. He didn't say it in so many words when I pinned him down in a second discussion, but it's evident that Don thinks it's his wife who is unstable and is using visitation rights with Bonnie as a weapon because she's jealous of the relationship between father and daughter. He has agreed to turn himself over peacefully to the authorities as soon as we get back to Baltimore. I think he feels defeated that the deck is stacked against him, and he traded this one chance at being with his daughter for his future freedom. It will be that lovely child who will bear the most scars from this, I'm afraid."

She went on to say, "I couldn't continue on the cruise keeping the situation a secret from you, Brenda. We've declared we'd minimize the secrets between us."

"Yes we have," Brenda agreed. "But isn't there anything else we can do for Don and Bonnie?"

"I've already done the most I think can be done," Charlotte said. "I've asked Evan Worthington to contract the best attorney for these matters on the East Coast that he can find and have him—or her—waiting for us and Don at dockside as soon as we arrive back in Baltimore."

The two women ran silent for several minutes, each thinking her own thoughts, and both lost in the quiet piano music—so much more quiet than that of all of the other bands playing in the many public areas of the ship.

"I do wish there was more we could do for him, though," Brenda said.

"Speaking of secrets," Charlotte said, changing the subject because she didn't see anything else that could be done for the Blaines, "the captain alluded to some secret he and Tony shared that we'd find out about later. You aren't in on that too, are you?"

"No. I wondered about that too. But for some reason I think Michelle knows what it is. She didn't seem a bit surprised when the captain mentioned it."

"Hum. So I guess it's Michelle we need to work on?"

"It does look that way, yes. But look, the cruise director is at the entrance to the bar, although he didn't see us and moved on. I doubt there's any secret about him. He's come to get me for the floor show, I'm sure. Will you be there to cheer me on?"

"You'd better believe it. From here on out it's you and me chained together," Charlotte answered. And she meant it in the best possible way, and she could tell by Brenda's laugh that she took it well too, but it was a very short time before Charlotte discovered how difficult that could be.

Brenda rose from her seat at the small, round cocktail table and said, "I guess I had better track down Eduard now and get last-minute instructions from the cruise director on what I'm supposed to do this evening. I will meet up with you later."

Charlotte—along with everyone else in the cocktail lounge—watched Brenda glide out of the room. Charlotte gave a little smile, though, knowing that it would only be her going to bed with Brenda that night. Or at least so she thought.

* * * *

The Neptune Theater was packed to the gills—so much so that Charlotte, rather prophetically, wondered if there were any fire codes about occupancy of a theater room on one of these ships. She had initially gone with Brenda backstage, which was practically nonexistent, the stage of the theater being almost right up against the stern of the ship on the fifth and sixth decks. By the time she had left Brenda, the theater was nearly full and it was still forty-five minutes before the show was to start. The only seat she could find was at the back of the sixth-deck balcony, as far away from the stage as possible. Marilyn and Chance were sitting in the middle of the orchestra seats and Michelle and Tony had given the show a pass, with Tony rather cryptically saying they had to prepare for the next day. It occurred to Charlotte that this meant that perhaps the surprise the captain and Tony had talked about was to be sprung the next day. Charlotte hoped so and that they'd quickly get past that little surprise; it would be one less mystery for her to stew about.

The Blaines also weren't there, Don saying that the show would be too late for Bonnie to be up. Charlotte applauded him for this—and for holding out against all of Bonnie's pleas—even though she could see plenty of children Bonnie's age and younger in the audience. Glen Welden had somehow snarfed up a front-row seat. Charlotte thought that perhaps he'd skipped dinner altogether and had arrived with the first invasion force, still saturated with worship for Brenda. She wondered, knowing that it was catty and marked the danger she saw in the man regarding her relationship with Brenda, whether he was sitting up front in hopes to be called up to the stage again to accept applause. She quickly dispelled this image, though, as something about the man seemed not to walk that much in the light.

Brenda was singing her third and last song, which had been inserted between two scenes involving extensive costume changes for the eight singers and dancers in the troupe—four men and four women—when all in the theater were alerted to danger by the first screams coming from those down in front who realized that the flames licking up the backdrop on the stage were not stage magic. They were real flames.

Pandemonium broke out. Charlotte, crying out Brenda's name and reaching out toward the stage, was pushed back by the surge of those stampeding toward the exits on either side of the theater behind her. There were just four exits, two on either side on each level, on just the one end of the hall, behind the seating, back toward the middle of the ship. The theater took up the full width of the ship at that point.

As the back wall of the stage started to give way, showing that the ocean was just beyond, Charlotte caught a glimpse of Glen Welden jumping up to the stage and pulling a startled and paralyzed Brenda down into the orchestra area before Charlotte herself was pushed out into the stairwell behind the theater and ultimately into the casino beyond. Here gamblers remained glued to slot machines seemingly unaware of the horde of screaming—and drenched, since the sprinklers in the theater had opened up immediately—people surging around them and trying to get as far away from the fire in the theater as possible.

Chapter Eight: Up the Creek Without a Paddle

While many of the theatergoers in the balcony were streaming back through the casino toward the bow of the ship and some were running up the stairs to the pool deck to be out in the open, Charlotte was one of the few pushing her way down the stairs. Few were taking this route because it would just lead them down to the mass of people trying to get out of the theater's main level.

But Charlotte was intent on being on that level to get to Brenda and to Chance and Marilyn, if she could. As people were escaping from the theater, crew members, carrying fire-fighting equipment, were moving as they could and as efficiently as possible toward the theater. Seeing their diminutive room attendant, Eleni Hernandez, and another small woman room attendant failing to make headway in the onslaught of people, Charlotte threw herself into the crowd, pulling the two behind her and acting as a formidable wedge into the fray. They parted at the entrance to the main level of the theater, as the crowd thinned and Charlotte almost ran into Chance and Marilyn.

"Charlotte, you're safe," Chance called out as the two room attendants, tossing their thanks at Charlotte over their shoulders, scooted around Brenda's brother and ran into the theater. There was smoke, but it wasn't too bad.

"Brenda?" Charlotte cried out.

"I don't know. We didn't see her," Chance answered, the concern on his face visibly deepening as, until now his concern had totally been for his wife.

"The fire's not that bad," Marilyn said, and although she coughed, she added. "There isn't much smoke, so Chance said we should wait to try to get out because getting trampled in the crowd was more of a danger than a fire that hadn't gotten beyond the stage curtains yet."

At that moment, the signal for the public address system came on and the voice of the captain could be heard saying, "There is no reason for alarm. There's been a fire on the stage of the Neptune Theater, but it's under control now. No station drill is being called, but all passengers, as well as all crew not attending the fire, are asked to go immediately to their cabins so that we can account for everyone. Again, the fire is contained and under control."

"We can go back and look for her," Chance said when the speaker went off.

"No, I'll go. You get Marilyn back to your cabin as instructed."

"And I'm afraid it's the same for you, madam," a rather determined senior-looking ship's officer said, barring the way, as best he could, into the theater, as Chance and Marilyn scurried off.

Trying to look around him, Charlotte said, "My wife was on stage. She may have been—"

The ship's officer looked at Charlotte like she might be in shock and delusional, but he said, "Beyond a couple of the dancers getting a little singed, there are no injuries that we have found yet. Look for yourself. The fire didn't get into the audience area."

"I am looking for Brenda Brandon, the movie star. She's my wife. She wasn't in the audience. She was singing on stage."

"As far as I know the only ones who received any injuries at all were a couple of the dancers. Everything is under control. It was only a minor fire."

"It looks like the flames opened the whole back of the ship open," Charlotte said. "That's hardly minor damage." And indeed, she was staring at rolling waves now beyond the back of what had been the stage area. "And, and as I said, Brenda Boynton—I mean Brandon," Charlotte corrected herself, using Brenda's stage name, "was on stage, singing. That's who I'm looking for. She could have fallen off the back of the ship."

This time the ship's officer seemed to actually listen to what Charlotte was saying.

"Ah, Ms. Brandon was helped off the stage by an elderly gentleman. I'm sure she's returned to her cabin—as you should do, madam, so that you won't be listed as a possible casualty. And the damage really isn't as serious as it looks. It's sort of an illusion. The back of the stage is right at the stern of the ship. There's only a narrow corridor in front of a glass rear. The fire blew out the glass. The damage is really not all that—"

A muffled explosion from deep under the stern that knocked Charlotte and the officer against each other and nearly off their feet cut short the man's assuring explanation. With effort, he helped Charlotte right herself, and he was now looking anything but assured. "Please return to your cabin now. I need to go check on something."

A second explosion knocked both against the wall as the officer moved away from Charlotte at nearly a dead run.

* * * *

Charlotte heard the low voices beyond the door to the suite as she was fumbling around with her sea pass card. She was both relieved and a bit irritated at the same time. She had no trouble picking out the voices of either Brenda or Glen Welden. Still, it was a shock when she opened the door to see Brenda sitting on a sofa and Glen Welden on an ottoman in front of her. Brenda, her hair dangling in wet strings, was wearing a bathrobe, which was pulled up to over her knees. Welden's hands were cupping a knee. He was still wearing the clothes he'd worn to the theater, and he was soaked as well.

If Charlotte could ever be speechless, she would have been then, but the closest she could come to that was in letting out no more than a deep "Oofff" sound.

Both Brenda's and Welden's heads shot up and turned toward the door. Welden had the decency to look both startled and embarrassed. Brenda just gave another one of her radiant, open smiles.

"Charlotte. I was worried about you, but here you are."

"Not as worried as I was about you," Charlotte shot back, her eyes obviously glued to Welden's hands as he slowly retracted them from Brenda's knee and had the decency to blush. "You were on stage. You should see it now. It's a mess."

"I'm not surprised," Brenda said. "I got soaked when the sprinklers came on. But Glen was my hero. He had me off the stage and halfway up the aisle to the back before anyone else in the hall had recovered enough to head toward the exits. Glen was magnificent."

"And is obviously getting his reward," Charlotte said dryly. Welden's embarrassed look deepened.

"Oh, the knee," Brenda said. Then she gave one of her tinkling laughs. "I wrenched my knee a bit. Glen was just checking it and massaging it a bit."

"Yes, I can see that." And making it all better—as much for him as for you, Charlotte added in her thoughts.

"Well, if you think it's better, perhaps I should be going," Welden said to Brenda.

"That probably would be best," Charlotte said, not giving Brenda a chance to invite him to stay longer. "You'll want to get into some dry clothes before you catch a cold. And you may not have heard the announcement. Everyone is to return to their cabin so they can be accounted for."

"Oh, that's not much of a problem for me," Welden said. "I best be going anyway, though. But I heard and felt two explosions, I thought."

"Yes," Charlotte answered, perplexed by why going to a cabin wouldn't be a problem for Welden and thinking that he had changed the subject rather abruptly. "It was quite pronounced in the stern. Like it was down in the engine room."

"Ah, maybe that's why we're not moving," Welden said.

For the first time Charlotte realized he was right. The ship wasn't moving. "Maybe they stopped to make sure the fire was out and to survey the damage."

"Or maybe—" Welden started to say, but there was a knock on the door. The rest of the party, Marilyn and Chance and Tony and Michelle were outside. Tony finished Welden's thought without realizing he had done so as he entered the room. "I flagged down one of the maintenance crew in the corridor as he was passing by. There's a problem in the engine room. We've lost power."

"Lost power?" Brenda said. "But the lights are still on and the air conditioning."

"Well, not all of the power, apparently," Tony said. "But we certainly aren't moving. We're dead in the water."

"Up the creek without a paddle," Brenda said in a low voice.

"Well, I must go," Welden repeated. No one answered or stopped him as he maneuvered around the four who had just arrived and not advanced very far into the cabin yet.

As he departed, though, the room attendant, Eleni Hernandez, entered, looking like she was in a panic.

"You must go immediately. Somewhere else. Right now, Ms. Brandon," she said, zeroing in on Brenda.

"But why?" Marilyn answered for all of them.

"You all must go. This suite isn't safe. Ms. Brandon isn't safe. They're here."

"Who's here, dear?" Brenda asked.

They all heard the thunk . . . out on the balcony.

"What the hell?" Chance exclaimed and took a step in that direction. But Tony was already on the move, through the sliding glass doors, and out onto the balcony.

"What is that?" Charlotte called out to Tony. "It looks like a—"

"It's a grappling hook. Lodged on the rail." Tony answered in a shocked voice. "What the . . . ? There are boats down there. Speed boats." With a jerk, he pulled the hook out of the rail and threw it back over the side. They all heard a couple of gunshots, and Tony staggered back toward the balcony doors. Brenda screamed.

"They're here. The pirates are here!" Eleni Hernandez screamed.

Chapter Nine: Dark Sanctuary

"Tony!" Michelle called out.

"I'm fine," Tony said, as he ducked back into the cabin. "The shots went over my head. As far as I can see, all of the other hooks with rope ladders have hooked into lower decks. I don't think they'll be up this high by that route any time soon."

"Pirates? How do you know they are pirates, Eleni?" Charlotte had seized the room attendant by her sleeve. "Does this have anything to do with the Hispanic young man I've seen you trying to avoid but who you were talking with in the doorway to the pool?"

"Ms. Diamond. You need to leave, to find somewhere else to go. Now. Ms. Brandon isn't safe."

"What do you mean Brenda isn't safe? Do these men intend to kidnap her?"

"Yes. I know one of the men. He's a bad man. I've tried to stay away from him for years. But he knew I was here. And he saw Ms. Brandon, and . . . and . . . he's with pirates. They planned to stop the ship and loot it. And when he saw Ms. Brandon, he decided they would take her too . . . for ransom. He told me this. He told me to find out where her cabin was."

"And you told him it was here?"

"No, my god, not that, no. I told him I didn't know where, but he told me to find out. I didn't tell him I was your room attendant. He'll find out from someone which suite is yours. It's in the records at reception. They already are on board. You have to go now."

"But where can we go?" Marilyn cried out.

"You all have to clear out. I turned back because there are bandits in the stair hall. They'll loot and they'll come right for the suites." The voice was that of Glen Welden, who had appeared in the doorway.

"But where could we go?" Tony said. "To our cabin or Chance and Marilyn's?"

"Those are junior suites and on this same corridor," Charlotte said. "They'll be among the first that are looted."

"I have a place you should be safe," Welden spoke up. "Down on deck two."

"But the pirates are in the stairway. We could never get past," Charlotte shot back. "And Brenda can't get far or fast with a wrenched knee."

"There's a crew staircase just across the hall. We'll go down that," Welden said. "And we'll carry Brenda if we have to."

They were filing out to the corridor as Charlotte continued to quiz the room attendant. "Is that true, Eleni?" Charlotte asked. "That there are crew staircases on the ship?"

"Yes. In the cross hallway just a few doors down," Eleni answered. "I will stay here and—"

"No, you will not," Charlotte answered as she latched onto Eleni's sleeve and pulled her toward the cross hallway. "You will be in danger too if you truly haven't helped the pirates. And if you have, you now know where we're going. Either way, you're coming with us." Then turning to Brenda, but was being held in a steadying embrace and helped down the corridor by Michelle, Charlotte said, almost tenderly, "Are you OK? Can you manage to get down six flights of stairs with help? We'll stick together and not hurry you any more than we have to."

Bracing herself up, Brenda put on a brave face and, as jauntily as she could manage, said, "Lead on MacDuff. I'd follow you to the ends of the earth, Charlotte."

Farther down the decks of the ship than Charlotte imagined even existed, Welden led them along a rather dim and dark hallway running through the ship toward the stern—certainly a lot less elegant than the corridors on the eighth-deck suite level. Then he made a sharp left, just before reaching one of the main stair ways, into a narrower corridor and then another left into an even dimmer and more confining hallway. He stopped in front of a door marked 2925.

"Just a jiff," he said. Charlotte was standing closest to him. Most of the others had their eyes cast back toward the direction they had come from. Welden took a credit card out of his wallet, inserted it into the door lock, and the door opened.

"Not really your cabin?" Charlotte asked, her eyebrows moving up her forehead.

"It's the cabin I use . . . it was one I found that's not occupied for this cruise. Even if the pirates obtain a manifest, there will be no indication there are passengers in this cabin. But it's the cabin I use."

"And you, Glen? Are you on the manifest for this cruise."

"Not exactly."

"Are you having a problem getting in?" Chance asked from in back of them.

"No, we're in," Charlotte answered in a stage whisper. "But we need to be very, very quiet." She decided that this was no time to start getting to the bottom of whatever Welden was up to on this cruise.

Both she and Welden stepped aside as the others filed past them and into a small interior cabin. It didn't take them long to look around and determine that most of them were going to have to find space to sit around the double bed that took up most of the cabin.

"I'm sorry that it isn't much," Welden said, "But you should all be safer here than up in higher decks. It shouldn't take the authorities long to realize our predicament and to send help."

"Yes, if the explosions we heard weren't knocking out the communications system as well as the motion engines," Chance said with a frown.

"After you," Charlotte said to Welden, after she'd nudged Chance not to volunteer more issues to worry about.

"No, you go ahead inside Charlotte," Welden responded. "I'm going to go get the Blaines if I can and bring them here too.

I know what cabin they're in, and it's just up a few decks from here. The little girl must be terrified. Being with Michelle and the others will keep her calm and occupied."

"You can't go out again. The pirates will find you. I'm sure they're being rough on anyone they find outside their cabin."

"I'm an old man. No one sees old men. If I've learned nothing else over the past few years, I've learned that—and counted on it. And the pirates will be concentrating up on the deck where your cabin is—that's where the valuables will be. I won't go through any public areas. I know the nooks and crannies of this ship like the back of my hand."

He was gone before Charlotte could pursue that point. When she entered the cabin and closed and bolted the door behind her, the men were continuing their conversation and the women were huddled on the bed and trying not to show how nervous they were.

"Even then, if the commo system has been knocked out, it will just be a matter of time before help arrives," Tony interjected, giving Chance a meaning-filled look and nodding his head toward the women. "Lack of communications is as much a signal to come looking for us as a distress signal would be."

"But that could be hours, maybe not until after daylight. And who knows how far out in the ocean we are anyway?" Chance said. He obviously hadn't gotten Tony's signal.

Tony shook his arm and muttered, "Cool it. The women." But the damage was already done.

"You were at the lecture this afternoon, Chance," Marilyn spoke up in a trembly voice. "We're in the Bermuda Triangle now. And we all know how ships have just vanished and never been seen again in the Bermuda Triangle."

"I don't think we're as offshore as that," Tony said, making a stab at containing the rising panic. "Those were speedboats I saw at the base of the ship. They can't have much range. I'm sure the pirates are doing a grab and go. They've come from somewhere not far off."

This might have been settling if Eleni Hernandez hadn't chosen that moment to break down. She started wailing, much of it in Spanish, but they got the gist that she thought this was all her fault.

"Why your fault?" Brenda asked, taking the young woman in her arms as they sat on the bed.

"I should have known. I should have known that Hector was planning something—and all those young men with him. Thugs, all of them. I was looking for my supervisor to warn him of the danger to you—that Hector wanted me to find your cabin for him—and then the fire broke out."

"But you didn't tell him where my cabin was," Brenda said in a soothing tone. "And you could have. And he hasn't found me. So, nothing is your fault."

This didn't prevent Eleni from beginning to bawl.

"Tissues or a handkerchief." Brenda called out. "Anyone have them? Eleni, please don't cry. And we need to be silent."

The men were feeling in their pockets without luck and Marilyn and Michelle were just then realizing that they didn't have their pocketbooks with them. They had evacuated the suite too quickly and had been too focused on just escaping to somewhere safer.

Charlotte was pacing the other side of the room, looking for evidence of a tissue box. She was moving toward the small bathroom but was opening drawers in the wall unit on her way. She almost exclaimed when she opened a lower drawer. She did stagger back a bit at what she saw. It very quickly hit her what it was—and everything instantaneously snapped into place on Welden's curious statements about not being on the manifest, this not being a cabin assigned to him, and knowing how to move around the ship unobtrusively.

The bottom drawer was packed with jewelry and watches and wallets. And small electronic devices as well.

She slammed the drawer closed, nearly stumbled into the bathroom, found the tissues, and was returning with a handful . . . when the lights went out. And the air conditioning went off, with the air immediately going stale in a small cabin not designed for seven nervous breathers being within the confines of four windowless walls.

They all held their breath for the longest second. The silence was broken by Chance whispering, "Shit. They must have cut the power too."

This was closely followed by the sound of the cabin door creaking open and the start of a scream by Eleni, which was stifled by Brenda's hand.

"Everyone OK?" Glen Welden asked. "I found them. Here, Bonnie, the bed is just to the right. Let me help you—"

"I'm right here, Bonnie, honey," Michelle said. "I'm holding my hand out. There, yes, that's it. Come sit with me."

"The power," Chance said. "We can't stay in this cabin long."

"I don't think we'll have to wait long," Welden said, "and I think they've stayed on the upper decks. I could see them scrambling when I came into the corridor on deck seven. And there was gunfire. I heard helicopter noise above the ship. They seemed to be shooting up in the air, so I don't think the helicopters belong to the pirates."

"Helicopters?" Tony asked in a shocked voice. "Oh, shit."

"I got the impression the pirates are already leaving the ship," Welden continued.

When everyone was settled down for what did, in fact, prove to be a short wait before the lights came back on, an "all clear" announcement was made over the public address system, and they could emerge from the cabin into a ship devoid of invading pirates, including Hector and the group he'd had on board, Charlotte pulled Welden over to near the bathroom door and whispered in his ear.

"After this, we'll have to talk," she whispered. "I've seen what you have in your bottom drawer."

"Ah, yes, I guessed you would have pieced it together," he answered in a dejected voice. "Just my luck to run smack dab into a copper on what was to be my last cruise."

* * * *

"So, I think it worked."

"Shhh. Yes, I think so too."

"I don't know how to thank you, Charlotte."

"For the moment you can thank me by sitting back in the chair and piping down. The ceremony's about to begin."

"Well, thank you again." Glen Welden started to lean back in the row behind the front row, where Charlotte and Brenda were sitting in the narrow row of chairs set out beside the pool on the ship's pool deck. But, as if by an afterthought, Charlotte turned, grabbed Welden's lapel, pulled his face close to hers, and said in a harsh whisper, "You can thank me by never, ever doing that again. And if you hadn't saved Brenda twice over we wouldn't be handling this this way."

"Yes, ma'am," a chastened Glen murmured and settled back in his chair.

"Thanking you for what?" Brenda asked, tearing her attention away from the small platform set out in front of the row of chairs.

"Oh, just because," Charlotte answered breezily. "Aren't they ready to start yet? The captain is in place."

Oh, just because, Charlotte thought. Because she was an old softy, and because the man was charming, because he'd returned everything he'd stolen on the cruise, and because she had no official duties anymore and could do as she pleased—and, yes, mostly because the man really had saved Brenda twice over, first from the fire on the stage and then by hiding her away from the pirates. He had done the greatest service for Charlotte that anyone could do—and on a day like this Charlotte was prepared to do just about anything for the man, even though she still got a clutchy feeling when she saw Brenda's and his heads together chatting about old times in the movies.

Charlotte actually hadn't thought it would work, but it did. She stayed behind for a few extra minutes in Welden's pilfered cabin and told him exactly what he'd have to do or she would turn him in for his pickpocketing activities on board.

"How long have you been doing this?" She asked.

"Three years," he said. "Someone showed me the ropes the first time, but since then it's been four cruises a year. I come on with the luggage handlers and then go looking for a cabin they aren't going to use. They have charts showing that in the attendants' work rooms. No one cards anyone at the Galleon Café as long as you just use the buffet. I take away enough from each cruise to keep me from starving between sailings—no more. I'm not a total schmuck. But it's the only way I have been able to survive. There was no such thing as a pension plan when I was working in Hollywood and I outlived what I'd saved. I had no idea I'd live this long. I shouldn't have."

"Yes, you should have," Charlotte said. "You stayed around to save Brenda. I can tell that that's worth it just by the way you look at her. Think about that. You stayed around to save her—twice."

Welden perked up at that. And then he went gloomy again. "But she'll hate me for what I've been doing—stealing from the passengers. I'm no better than the pirates."

"You are if you just stop it now. And there's no reason Brenda—or anyone else—needs to know, if we can prevent it. And I can't turn you in after what you've done for us all today. But you've got to give all of it back."

"Give it back? Sure, that's OK with me. But how can I do that?"

"We'll find a sack—wearing gloves. I'll go do that while you wipe all of the stuff clean."

"I kept it wiped clean."

"Good. Then when I get back, it all goes in the sack, and then we're leaving the sack at the railing somewhere close to where the pirates jumped ship. It will look like they gathered it from somewhere and then dropped it in their hasty escape. It's a thin plan, but the owners will be so happy to get it back that I doubt any of them will pay much attention to how tenuously the dots connect. They'll be happy to think it was Hector and his crew who were stealing it from the first day in the terminal."

They'd quickly put the plan into action and it worked a charm.

So, one problem down, Charlotte thought, as she looked across the aisle to where Don Blaine sat and tried to gauge how that situation was working out.

"It's me who should be thanking Glen." Brenda's whisper brought Charlotte's attention back to the ceremony, which now

98

seemed to be in some sort of delay, but she knew not to bite her fingernails over it; these affairs usually started late. Her first one certainly had.

"I think just that you have treated him so decently is thanks enough," Charlotte answered. "He obviously worships you."

"I think he's poor as a dormouse. I can't imagine how he manages to come on the cruises he has."

"Yes, it's certainly hard to imagine how he manages," Charlotte whispered back, trying to keep a straight face.

"I've offered him a room at Curtain Call," Brenda said, referring to the rest home for indigent movie folks that she and Charlotte had established in Hopewell. "He's the ideal candidate for a full-stipend resident."

"That's right, he is. Good decision." It was all Charlotte could do to keep from clinching her teeth. It was, in fact, perfectly logical. Why hadn't she thought of the possibility?

"But?" Brenda leaned over and asked. "There seems to be a but there. Oh, I see. You think he's sweet on me and there's a danger I'll be sweet on him." She laughed, and everyone sitting and waiting for the ceremony to begin turned to look toward her. Everyone knew exactly whose laugh that was.

"Something like that, I'm afraid," Charlotte answered.

"So you're afraid about my habit of falling in love with gay men," Brenda said, with a teasing smile. She was referring to the leading man in many of her films, the now-deceased David Runion, who Brenda had waited for for several decades without realizing he was gay.

"Gay? Glen is gay?" Charlotte almost said it loud enough for others to hear—but not quite. They heard that she'd said something, but, thankfully, the procession music had started just then and covered her exclamation.

"Of course he is, sweetie," Brenda answered. "There's no threat there whatsoever," and she stood with the others to watch her son, Tony, coming down the aisle, with his soon-to-be bride, Michelle Minor, on his arm. That they walked together was against tradition, of course, but no one present cared about tradition when a surprise wedding was being conducted on board a crippled cruise ship being towed toward the Bahamas by tugs and already within sight of the towers of the Atlantis resort on Nassau's Paradise Island, near the dock the ship was being towed to.

As the couple reached the first row of seats, their flower girl, a beaming Bonnie Blaine, leading the way, Tony stopped to offer his arm to Brenda as she stood and they proceeded to stand in front of the captain for the official marriage ceremony.

Although the confusion and drama of the moment in Glen Welden's purloined cabin had short circuited noting how incongruous Tony's "Oh, shit" exclamation at hearing that helicopters were hovering over the pirate-seized cruise ship was, sometime after dawn following the departure of the pirates Tony owned up that this was connected with the surprise that had been alluded to at the captain's dinner.

Tony had decided to ride on his mother's coattails and got Michelle to agree to marry him on board the cruise liner as it approached the Bahamas, where they would leave the ship and have their honeymoon at the Atlantis resort.

The helicopters that stirred up the pirates had been transporting some two dozen wedding guests who were to drop in for a surprise visit to Brenda and Charlotte. The guests' helicopters scooted back to the Bahamas, knowing something was wrong when they were being fired upon and a bunch of speedboats were lashed to the sides of the ship. The next round of helicopters and Coast Guard ships, alerted by the wedding guests, arrived soon afterward but not before the pirates retreated to their speedboats and started to make their getaway. The pirates hadn't counted on rescuers showing up so fast or that the rescuers wouldn't all just stay at the ship, however. The speedboats were followed to the pirates' lair on one of the thousands of small, supposedly deserted Bahamian islands, and the pirates were apprehended.

When the wedding party helicopters returned, the passengers aboard included the movie producer, Aaron Woolridge, and director, Howard Holton, who had worked on many films together with both Brenda and Tony.

As a surprise to all of Brenda and Charlotte's party, the passenger list of the wedding helicopters also included the name of Ginny Blaine. Before Brenda had gone off to sing on a stage made fiery, thanks to a tribe of pirates, she had gone to the cruise director, who had helped her get in touch with Aaron Woolridge.

Explaining the plight of Don Blaine to him, Brenda had asked Woolridge, "Is there anything else we could do for this man? I hate to see him thrown in jail just because he took his daughter—a young girl who worships him—on the cruise she wanted to go on and his wife held back permission and then charged Don with kidnapping just to punish the girl's father."

"I'll see what I can produce," Woolridge had answered. And produce he did, immediately. It turned out that Mrs. Blaine was dying to get into the movies. A fast background actor contract later and Ginny Blaine was on a helicopter, agreeing to drop all charges against her husband and to allow very generous visitation rights for her estranged husband with Bonnie.

Bonnie didn't care what arrangements had been made— she didn't even know the lengths to which the wrangling had gone on; she just was delighted to see her parents together and being cordial to each other, even though she accepted that they weren't getting back together. Brenda and Charlotte hoped the young girl would never know what a sacrifice her father had been willing to make to give her this dream cruise or how quickly her mother had grasped for a brass ring and dropped all pretenses of being worried that her daughter was with her estranged husband.

The two Blaines were sitting side by side at the ceremony, but each in a world of their own, although the eyes of both followed Bonnie down the aisle in her combined role as bridesmaid and flower girl. Don looked relieved and Ginny looked smug. Charlotte only hoped that Ginny's career on the West Coast would mean that she would leave Bonnie in Don's care on the East Coast for prolonged periods, as there was no question which one was more the loving parent. She was pretty sure the "career" would be prolonged, because Aaron Woolridge knew what was needed and had both the clout and the heart to get it done.

Charlotte, whose judgment was not questioned, was able to smooth everything over with the authorities who had been looking for Don Blaine.

Brenda came back when she had given her son away to sink into the chair with Charlotte for the recessional. There were tears of joy in her eyes that Charlotte reached over and brushed away.

"No one can say my son has bad judgment. He picked the best to marry."

"Granted," Charlotte said dryly, "But he tried out a whole lot of duds en route."

Brenda laughed. Then she tried to look more serious, the women still sitting there, as the rest of the guests prepared to go up to the Mermaid Lounge at the top of the ship for the reception. Those in the wedding party were virtually the only passengers left on board as the cruise ship was being towed into Nassau harbor for extensive repairs. Most of the rest of the passengers had been happy to take the deal to be shuttled back to Cape Canaveral by helicopter and thence by plane back to their cars in Baltimore, with a full refund on this cruise and a chit for a free future cruise in their purses—and the prospect of having a fascinating, celebrity studded yarn to regale their family and friends with for years to come.

"It turned out very nice in the end, Charlotte. You'll have to acknowledge that. You can stop calling it our horrid honeymoon now. And the cruise line and Atlantis are giving us a four-day complimentary stay at the resort. The honeymoon will just be a little late. It will be wonderful from here on out."

"Don't say that," Charlotte said. "You might jinx our chances of getting over this last little stretch of water into the harbor without incident."

"You really did have your hands full with mysteries on this cruise, didn't you?" Brenda asked.

"And you really aren't going to get away with a full complimentary stay at Atlantis," Charlotte countered. "As soon as the resort has you in their clutches, they'll have you on stage and in reception lines. You realize that, don't you?"

Brenda sighed. "Yes, of course I realize it. But it's what I do, Charlotte. Just like sleuthing is what you do. That's the best part of coming together at our age. We can be fully devoted to each other without losing who we are individually. Don't you agree?"

"Yes, I suppose so," Charlotte said. "But there's something I want to see in documentation."

"What is that, love?"

"Before you move to letting Glen Welden settle in at Curtain Call, I want to see some sort of signed affidavit proving that he's gay and isn't going to be trying to take you away from me."

Both women were laughing as, arm in arm, they walked back up the aisle toward the stairs up to the Mermaid Lounge.

Chapter Ten: Putting the Last Mystery to Bed

The slip of paper in Charlotte's hand had led her west to Frederick, Maryland, and Hood College. She was forced to almost beat the information out of the FBI Annapolis chief, Even Worthington, when she and Brenda returned from what Charlotte was still characterizing as "the horrid honeymoon," despite all of the good things that Brenda kept pointing out had come out of that week.

In the end she had to give Evan a "maybe" on doing official consulting work with the Bureau. It had been with great fear and trepidation that she had approached telling Brenda she might go back to work for the Bureau part time, which wasn't helped when Brenda laughed and said, "Of course you are. We both know that you really want to do it. And you should." It didn't help that Evan had said much the same thing to her—or that, deep down, she realized it was true.

When they returned to Hopewell and after Charlotte ascertained from Evonne Clagett at the Curtain Call retirement community that Zenna Brodsky had not returned to work and that Evonne had had to replace her with someone doing a good job—"But it's just not Zenna"—Charlotte had gone to Zenna's home. The place was empty. Then she'd checked out Grady Tarbell's house too. It also was empty. And the houses weren't just empty. They had "For Sale" signs on them. The Realtor was one Charlotte had already worked with, not necessarily happily,

Scooter Wilson. Checking with her led nowhere, either because Scooter was under a gag order or she just didn't want to help Charlotte. Either was equally plausible.

So, Charlotte went to Evan, who showed delight at seeing her but who was only helpful because Charlotte could read between the lines.

"The Talbot County police are acting like there wasn't even a murder of a Russian diplomat in Hopewell," Charlotte said. "Or that Zenna Brodsky and Grady Tarbell ever existed."

"Imagine that," Evan said.

"There's been some sort of deal with the Russians, hasn't there? They got caught red-handed and it isn't any more in their interests to talk about a Russian diplomat or three—because there were two others; they upset my wedding by driving off with our limousine—being in Hopewell than there is for the U.S. authorities to be talking about a dead Russian diplomat, is there?"

"Foreign relations are certainly complicated," Evan said. "Some things are larger than Talbot County—and larger even than the FBI."

"At least tell me that Zenna is safe, Evan. And Grady Tarbell. We care about them in Hopewell. I'm the town's mayor; I feel some responsibility for them, besides which Zenna is a good friend of mine. I knew Win Engleton had salted Zenna away in Hopewell and was looking out for her until he disappeared. She must have done something really significant for the United States in Russia to receive that sort of care."

"One would think so, yes."

"Something so outrageous to the Russians that they would continue to try to find her. I can't just let this go on Zenna, Evan."

"I think you can, Charlotte. I think the Russians have."

"What do you mean?"

"The Russians wouldn't be interested if Zenna was no more," he said.

"No more? No more what? You're not saying she's dead then? You're saying she's safe? Given a new life?"

"I'm saying that I certainly wish you'd come back and take up your top secret clearance and work with us again, Charlotte.

Then maybe you'd know more than I can tell you. Beyond that I can't say anything. You know I can't. You were in the game yourself. And now, how about that lunch with your former colleagues? Everyone is anxious to hear about how your honeymoon went."

"I think you know how much of a muddle most of my horrid honeymoon was," Charlotte said, rising from her chair in front of Worthington's desk as he went around to take her coat off a hook and to help her into it. "It seems I can't get away from mysteries."

"You seem not to be able to get away from mysteries that you solve, Charlotte. This was just the sort of honeymoon your colleagues would enjoy hearing about. And it's precisely the reason you should sign back on as a consultant."

It was only later, after she'd returned to Hopewell and was taking her coat off, that Charlotte found the slip of paper Evan obviously had put in her pocket. It was merely an address, for the History Department, including an office room number, of the small Hood College in historic Frederick, Maryland. Charlotte understood instantly that Evan was going outside protocol—that he was leading her to Grady Tarbell, who had quit his position as a history professor at Washington College in Chestertown, not far from Hopewell.

She found Grady Tarbell in his office at Hood College. She hadn't called ahead and she doubted that Evan Worthington had warned him either, because he gave her a shocked look edged with guilt when he looked up and saw her standing in the doorway.

"Charlotte!" he exclaimed.

"Hello, Grady. We were worried about you and Zenna. I had to check for myself."

Now he looked scared, and it occurred to her that he had every reason to be frightened. From his perspective, if Charlotte could track Zenna this far, so could the Russians if they wanted to.

"Not to worry," she quickly said. "I just needed to check on you. I obtained the contact information from a highly controlled source. You must know that I have connections—

connections the Russians won't have, although I'm assured that they have reason to have given up. Just tell me that Zenna is OK. Her friends worry about her."

"I have no idea where Zenna might be. I have nothing to do with her. I was told she had died."

Charlotte looked down at the surface of Grady's desk where, next to a stack of papers he was grading, she saw a pastry on a napkin next to a half-filled cup of coffee. Grady's eyes went to the pastry as well. There was no need for words. Zenna had operated a bakery in Hopewell. Her pastries were quite distinctive.

"I have to go to a meeting across campus," Grady said. "Perhaps you'll walk with me and you can fill me in on how life is in Hopewell."

Charlotte caught what he was saying—that he didn't want to talk about any of this in his office. She didn't really think he was overreacting, under the circumstances, to the possibility that someone was listening in on what was said in his office.

They walked down a typical, bucolic college town lane for a couple of blocks before Grady said anything. He stopped beside a picket fence in front of a comfortable-looking brick colonial that was much the same as the comfortable-looking brick colonials with picket fences everywhere on the block. In the next yard over, a woman was kneeling at a well-tended flower bed along the front of the house and was tending to it. Across the street an elderly man was cutting grass with a manual mower. Charlotte had the impression that perhaps the noise of a power mower wasn't accepted in the neighborhood. Farther down the block, another woman was watering hanging plants on her front porch.

"I killed him, the Russian," Grady abruptly said. "I'd never done anything like that before in my life. And I got away with it, and they said it shouldn't bother me under the circumstances, but there are days that it just tears me apart, Charlotte."

"They?" Charlotte asked.

"You know who. I don't think I need to spell it out for you."

"As I understand it, I don't think you should make yourself sick, Grady. I understand the circumstances, and the fact that it disturbs you, despite that you did it to save a precious life, is to your credit."

Grady gave her a sharp look but didn't say anything for a few minutes, during which Charlotte looked around the neighborhood, liking what she saw, the peaceful nature of it and the women tending their plants and man mowing his yard. It all looked so . . . right.

"You knew then," he finally said. "They told you or you figured it out?"

"I really haven't been told much of anything despite being allowed to find you—and that wasn't official, Grady. I would appreciate it if you didn't tell anyone about that. I guess you could say I figured it out. Was your accident by the Vales' B&B the snowy night of my wedding staged? How much of what happened was planned."

"No, the accident wasn't planned. Zenna called me in a panic from her home. Men were outside. She thought they were Russians. She hadn't even felt all that safe when Win Engleton was in town to protect her. There had been Russians sniffing around even then. She was very worried once he disappeared. But there wasn't anywhere she could go. I guess you could say that that helped in getting us together. She felt I gave her some protection. She called, and I was on the road, coming home from Chestertown, although I had been thinking of just pulling off the road because the snow was coming down so heavily—but, of course, I couldn't stop. Zenna needed me. Receiving the call from her didn't help my driving. I plowed into a tree near the B&B."

"And you saw the Russians dragging Zenna into the B&B?"

"Yes. Both of the Vales were in back of the house, shoveling snow on the parking lot. When I came out of my car, I saw the Russians manhandling Zenna up the stairs to the B&B. I carry a handgun in my car. I'm sure you can guess the rest. I shot one of the Russians, who had wrestled Zenna to an upstairs room. Afterward, I saw they had a hypodermic needle prepared. I still don't know if that was to drug her or kill her. I just panicked and shot the one who was struggling with her. Two of the Russians got away and I followed around to the side of the house, keeping back so that Joyce and Todd didn't see me. I could see them down the street in front of the church, knocking that young man who runs the filling station out and stealing the limousine. When they were gone, I walked Zenna back to my house—thinking any Russians still around wouldn't look for her there. Then I quickly came back, approached the Vales, telling them about my car accident, and they invited me to stay for dinner. You can only imagine how nervous I was and how hard it was for me to control those nerves until one of the Vales found the body upstairs. I was relieved that it was Todd, and not Joyce who did so."

"Then you took Zenna back to the apartment you kept at Washington College, in Chestertown?"

"Yes, a few days later, when the snow was cleared. But it didn't take the FBI long to take over the case of the dead Russian and to figure out what happened. By then the CIA was looking for their hidden asset, Zenna, too. It was all hushed up. They managed to cobble up a story for the Russians that Zenna had been killed too, and an agreement was struck on neither side making any of it public."

"Yes, that all makes sense," Charlotte said.

"But I got away with murder."

"You shouldn't see it that way, Grady. You got away with protecting Zenna from harm. Are you sure she's safe, though?"

Grady gave a little smile. "I figure if you, super sleuth that you are, can have stood here for ten minutes and not have recognized the changes in her appearance, the Russians won't find it easy."

"Ah," Charlotte said, looking more closely at the woman tending her garden in the neighboring house. No, she wouldn't have recognized her. That gave her comfort and hope. "I see. You might, though, suggest that new recipes be sought in making pastries."

"Point taken," Grady said.

* * * *

"We settled Glen in his Curtain Call room today."

The two women were sitting in Adirondack chairs near the banks of the Choptank River behind their colonial brick plantation house in Hopewell. Rocket had his head in Brenda's lap and Sam was rubbing up against Charlotte's legs as she brushed him. If dogs could purr with contentment, those boys were doing so.

"That's good to hear. Everything else OK at the retirement community?"

"Evonne, as always, has everything under control. She says, though, that she misses Zenna something terrible. And I do as well. I hope she is well and settled in another life."

"I'm sure she's doing fine," Charlotte answered.

Brenda turned and gave Charlotte a meaningful stare over the rim of her reading glasses. "You're telling me that she's OK, aren't you?"

Charlotte smiled, which is all Brenda really needed to know, and just repeated, "I'm sure she's doing fine."

"I'm glad to hear that," Brenda said. "I think Glen Welden's going to do fine at Curtain Call too. I'm delighted that we ran into him on the cruise—and not just because he was a lifesaver. When I envisioned creating Curtain Call with what I won from the Maryland lottery, it was exactly movie world people like Glen I was thinking of. I have no idea how he managed to live all these years since he was employed in Hollywood."

"Just tell Evonne to count the silverware after every meal," Charlotte said dryly.

Brenda welled up into a tinkling laugh. Charlotte didn't join her. She just looked up from brushing Sam and gave Brenda a steady look.

Brenda's laugh stopped. "You're serious, aren't you?"

"I'd just tell Evonne that, if I were you."

Brenda sighed. "Oh well, I've found that all of our residents there have a quirk or two. I've always known that you had to be half nuts to work in movies to begin with. What's that on the arm of your chair?"

"A letter from Jacksonville. It came today."

"Jacksonville? From Don Blaine?"

"Yes. He had tragic news."

"Tragic? Bonnie's OK, isn't she?"

"Oh, yes." And then Charlotte laughed. Not being used to hearing his mistress laugh, Sam looked up at her and put a paw in her lap. Charlotte nuzzled his face with hers, and Sam gave a little snort that almost sounded like a laugh of his own. "The tragedy is that Aaron has Ginny Blaine so tied up in crowd scene work in Hollywood that she's had to transfer custody of Bonnie to Don. She says she couldn't get enough time off work to supervise Bonnie even if she was moved out to California."

"Oh, how terrible," Brenda said in mock horror. "But how will Don manage to keep track of Bonnie? He works hard as an architect, doesn't he?"

"That's the other tragedy. Bonnie and Eleni Hernandez hit it off real well on the ship. Don hired Eleni as a live-in housekeeper. He says he feels like they're living between the covers of a *House Beautiful* magazine, Eleni is so meticulous. But Bonnie seems to love having Eleni there."

The women sat in silence for several minutes, sipping on the wine and watching the sun go down beyond the opposite banks of the Choptank. Brenda sighed.

"You know it wasn't a horrid honeymoon at all, Charlotte. It was rather nice and so much that was good happened. It was wonderful for Tony finally to get married. And to such a wonderful girl. He says, though, that he's going to have to cut back on his movie work. He says he's going wherever Michelle goes, and she travels all over the world on the pro tennis circuit."

"They'll be fine, yes," Charlotte answered. "And they're lucky to have each other. Not quite as lucky as I am to have you, though."

Brenda turned her face to Charlotte, smiled, and reached out an arm. Charlotte took her hand and squeezed it a bit.

"You know we deserve a real honeymoon," Brenda said.

Charlotte groaned. "Not another one like that, though, please. And I have a requirement for the next one."

"Oh, what?"

"Next time we take Sam and Rocket. I'm tired of leaving them home. The next honeymoon has to be a full-family deal."

"Deal!" Brenda exclaimed.

Both dogs rose up on their haunches and barked—just as if they understood what Brenda had said rather than only being set off by the tone of her exclamation.

~

About the Author

Olivia Stowe is a published author under different names and in other dimensions of fiction and nonfiction and lives quietly in a university town with an indulgent spouse.

You can find Olivia at www.CyberworldPublishing.com.

Our authors like to receive feedback and appreciate reviews being posted at distributor sites, Goodreads and other review sites.

Olivia Stowe at Cyberworld Publishing

Mystery Romance
Restoring the Castle

The Charlotte Diamond mystery series
By The Howling
Retired with Prejudice
Coast to Coast
An Inconvenient Death
What's The Point?
White Orchid Found
Curtain Call (Book 7)
Horrid Honeymoon (Book 8)

Making Room at Christmas (Seasonal Special)
Charlotte Diamond Mysteries Bundle 1 (Books 1&2)
Charlotte Diamond Mysteries Bundle 2 (Books 3&4)
Charlotte Diamond Mysteries Bundle 3 (Books 5&6)

The Savannah Series
Chatham Square
Savannah Time

Olivia's Inspirational Christmas collections
Christmas Seconds (2011)
Spirit of Christmas (2010)

www.ingramcontent.com/pod-product-compliance
Lightning Source LLC
Chambersburg PA
CBHW071327130626
46556CB00004B/1780